NOW Z

Lucas and Nina rar
landing.

They could see the Passmores on the ferry, all three of them, looking back toward North Harbor.

"Zoey!" Lucas shouted as loud as he could. "Zoey!"

"Zo!" Nina screamed next to him.

Zoey couldn't have failed to hear them, much less see them, but she gave no sign. She simply stood there, looking at them, her fair hair blowing in the wind. The look of sadness on her face was indescribable.

"Zoey!" Lucas shouted again, although he knew it was pointless.

It was over. She was gone.

Titles in the MAKING OUT series

1. Zoey fools around
2. Jake finds out
3. Nina won't tell
4. Ben's in love
5. Claire gets caught
6. What Zoey saw
7. Lucas gets hurt
8. Aisha goes wild
9. Zoey plays games
10. Nina shapes up
11. Ben takes a chance
12. Claire can't lose
13. Don't tell Zoey
14. Aaron lets go
15. Who loves Kate?
16. Lara gets even
17. Two-timing Aisha
18. Zoey speaks out
19. Kate finds love
20. Never trust Lara
21. Trouble with Aaron
22. Always loving Zoey
23. Lara gets lucky
24. Now Zoey's alone

Coming soon

25. Don't forget Lara
26. Zoey's broken heart

MAKING OUT

Now Zoey's alone

KATHERINE APPLEGATE

Pan Books

Cover photography by Jutta Klee

First published 1997 by Macmillan Children's Books
a division of Macmillan Publishers Limited
25 Eccleston Place, London SW1W 9NF
and Basingstoke

Associated companies throughout the world

ISBN 0 330 35119 2

1 3 5 7 9 8 6 4 2

A CIP catalogue record for this book is available from
the British Library.

Printed and bound in Great Britain by
Mackays of Chatham plc, Kent

Joey

What do I expect from next year? I expect to do a lot of surfing. I expect to meet a lot of new people. And I expect to miss my best friend and the love of my life.

Getting what you want can be a total mixed blessing. I really want to go to school in California; it's what I've always wanted. But suddenly I'm starting to wonder why in the world I ever wanted that so badly. What am I doing? Do I really have to go so far away?

There are moments when I'm sure of what I'm doing. In fact, I'm sure all the time. I's just that forty percent of the time I'm sure I'm making a mistake, and sixty percent of the time I'm sure I'm doing the right thing.

I know it sounds weird, but I wish that things weren't so perfect here. This island is full of people I love. Will I ever meet anyone as stable and kind as Lucas? Will I ever meet anyone as quirky and lovable as Nina? Do I even want to? It's strange, but the thought of making new friends doesn't really appeal to me. I love the ones I have. Nobody could ever take their place.

I have been thinking a lot about Lucas lately. I

want to spend time with him this week, doing whatever he wants to do. I want him to know how I feel about him.

But . . . there's a life waiting for me. I love these people, but there are so many things I want to do.

And I can't stay on this island forever.

Nina

I need to work on my outlook; I think I've been too negative about this whole "All My Friends Are Going Off to College" thing. I need to be more optimistic.

I think I'll use next year to build my image as Unbelievably Sexy Woman of Mystery. I'll change my name to something like Simona Van Damme and dress like Courtney Love, now that she's ~~sold out~~ changed her image. I can see it now: I stand sultrily in the cafeteria line. I request a chili dog, cooked medium well. Everyone stops. Everyone stares. Everyone says: who is that Unbelievably Sexy woman of Mystery?

And whatever happened to that Unbelievably Spazzy woman of Misery, Nina Geiger?

And I will chuckle to myself: Ha, ha! Nobody will guess my secret identity!

That's the beauty of having no friends. There's nobody to mess up your image!

Maybe I'll do what Claire did: sell my soul to the devil in exchange for beauty. It's faster and easier than a makeover. That way maybe I could take over her role as president of the After-School Satan-worshiping Society. Somebody has to run the coven. Otherwise the whole place might fall apart.

What an incredible opportunity; I'm really excited about a whole new year of school. And I'm sure that it will be the usual fascinating challenge: I can hardly wait to find out who won World War II! Perhaps I'll learn to conjugate Spanish verbs in the future tense! And maybe this year they will reveal who wrote Othello!

I have so much to look forward to that it makes me want to puke.

Aisha

I was so excited about next year, it's ridiculous. My future is all set: I'm going off to college, and I'm engaged to the man of my dreams. There is something very comforting about having your life all planned out.

The only problem with having such a clear plan is that it never quite turns out how you expected. Take, as an example right off the top of my head, the man of my dreams part of the equation. I never suffered under the illusion that Christopher was perfect. I just thought that he was perfect for me.

But it turns out that he isn't. Wasn't. It turns out that (a) he was married before, (b) the woman he was married to is a heroin addict, and (c) his former wife has a baby that may or may not be his. These are what we call Issues.

The fact is that they wouldn't be such big issues if Christopher would just talk to me about them. But he won't. And I don't understand why.

It makes me wonder whether he is hiding something even worse.

One

The bus from Boston dropped Aisha at the Weymouth station and departed with a loud whoosh of brakes and a gust of hot exhaust fumes that might have fluttered her clothes and hair if her clothes hadn't been so limp and wrinkled and her hair so sweaty and tangled.

She was wearing a long Indian-print skirt that clung sweatily to the backs of her legs. Her sleeveless white blouse had started out crisp and snowy, but now it looked like a used dinner napkin.

Aisha didn't care.

She walked slowly toward the ferry landing. She felt something on her cheek and touched her face absently. A tear. She flicked it away. She had been doing that for hours, producing one or two tears every ten minutes without even being aware of it. Not actually crying, really, but enough to make her look especially pathetic, she supposed.

I wonder how long this will continue, she

thought. *Maybe it's lifelong. Hopefully by the time I'm fifty, I'll be used to it.*

She had to run the last few steps to catch the ferry. Her sandaled feet slipped on the metal deck as the gate clanged up behind her. She moved toward the railing.

Even on the ferry there was no breeze. Aisha piled her curly dark hair on top of her head and held it there. Her black eyes were distant and preoccupied.

She was leaving for college in a few weeks. That meant she had to avoid Christopher for several hundred hours. Aisha's tired mind considered this. She once read that the average woman spent seventy-two hours shaving her legs over the course of a lifetime. When she first read that, Aisha thought, *That's not even possible—nobody's that vain,* but later she did the math during a particularly boring history class and it actually only worked out to something like forty-five seconds a day.

Okay, so she would fill forty-five seconds every day by shaving her legs. She was sure that if she stretched it out, she could make it last at least fifty-seven seconds. Another eight hours per day sleeping. Except that Aisha wasn't sleeping too well these days. But she could at least stay in bed for eight hours. Another two hours per day eating. Except . . .

well, Aisha wasn't eating very well, either. In fact, she'd lost four pounds in the past two days, and her already thin figure was beginning to look gaunt.

Aisha let her hair fall back onto her clammy neck and felt her protruding collarbones with her fingertips. *I have to get away,* she thought. *I have to somehow fill up this last horrible week, and then I can escape off to Princeton and never look back.*

Another tear slipped out of her eye. She caught it while it was still on her lashes. *Who is this man I was going to marry?* she wondered. She just didn't know anymore.

The ferry pulled up to the North Harbor landing, and Aisha automatically moved forward. Although she was grimy and sticky, even the thought of a long hot shower wasn't inviting. Nothing sounded appealing to her.

Aisha sighed. *I used to love baths,* she thought. *I used to love sleeping and eating, for that matter. I used to take pleasure in all sorts of things before Christopher ruined it all. Oh please please please let me leave without seeing him again.*

Claire sat at the breakfast bar in the kitchen, eating an apple and drinking a glass of milk. Her sister, Nina, and father, Burke Geiger, were sitting at the table. Claire's stepmother, Sarah, was upstairs getting dressed.

"I don't know how you can eat that," Burke said, watching Nina add sugar and honey to her mashed banana. "It's so—sweet."

"That's basically the point, Dad," Nina said. Her wide gray eyes were still sleepy, and her short, reddish brown hair stuck up in spikes. "I don't know how you can eat *that,*" she went on, indicating his bran flakes. "It's so—healthy."

Lying in front of Claire on the breakfast bar was a book titled *Captain Jack's Book of Self-defense.* Although *book* was probably overstating the case somewhat. It was more like a leaflet, considering that it was stapled, not bound, and it had a lot of typos. But it was the only book on self-defense that Claire found at the Weymouth public library.

Claire was writing an imaginary letter to Captain Jack.

Dear Captain Jack, it began. *I am only one chapter into your book and have already concluded that you are a sexist pig. . . .*

It said on the back of the book that Captain Jack was a former marine. Claire guessed that he had been too busy learning ways to kill people to participate much in the feminist movement.

"Claire, what are you doing today?" Burke asked.

"Shopping," Claire answered automatically. "I need some more stuff for school."

Nina made a little moaning sound.

"Imagine," Burke said. "Next week it'll be just you and me, Nina."

Nina moaned louder.

Claire continued. . . . *The term is* women, *for your information, unless you are speaking about a young child, and then the correct term is* girl. "Gal" *is grammatically incorrect and offensive.* "Little lady" *is just as obnoxious. . . .*

"Are you going to drive down to Cambridge with Claire and me?" Burke asked Nina.

"I guess," Nina said, spooning sugar into her bowl endlessly. "As long as you promise to leave me there."

Burke rolled his eyes. "Nina, I don't know why you're so upset about everyone else going to college. You can use this last year of high school to work hard and get into a good college like your sister."

"Like my who?" Nina raised her eyebrows.

"Your sister," Burke repeated.

"I don't have a sister."

"Nina—" Burke looked exasperated.

"I have an impostor you try to pass off as my sister. My real sister is probably at the bottom of Big Bite Pond."

Claire ignored this.

. . . Setting aside your sexist attitude, I have to tell you that your book has been very helpful. Yours, Claire Geiger.

The phone rang. None of them moved to answer it. It would only be the crank caller again. The same crank caller who had been calling Claire for weeks. And sent her notes and ominous photographs. And slashed the entire contents of her closet to ribbons. Burke and Nina only knew about the phone calls. They didn't know any of the rest. No one knew except Claire. And now Benjamin.

Claire reread the first part of chapter one:

Self-defense training is a waste of time for most gals. Most of them would do better with a plain old-fashioned hammer since most gals can use a hammer and are comfortable with it. And a hammer can do just as much damage to an intruder as any of the more advanced moves gals usually have trouble with. My advice is: Go to the hardware store, little lady.

Claire closed the leaflet and slipped it into her purse. She stood up, sliding the shoulder strap over her arm. "I'll take the ferry with you if you like, Dad," she said.

"Okay," Burke said, pushing back his chair. He went to the closet for his briefcase. "Oh, hey,

I tried to hang a picture last night and couldn't find my hammer. Have either of you—"

"Yeah, that's right," Nina said, her voice dripping with sarcasm. "We stole your hammer, Dad. Claire and I are going to build a tree house."

Claire said nothing. She patted her purse and smiled to herself.

Two

Zoey had to trot to keep up with Benjamin on their way to the beach, even though he was carrying a surfboard under his arm.

"I still can't believe how long it took you to get ready," he said for the fifth or sixth time. "It's lucky we made the ferry." There was a great beach in Weymouth where Benjamin liked to surf.

"I was trying to decide what to wear," Zoey said.

Benjamin rolled his eyes. "Look, we're going surfing, you wear a swimsuit. It's simple. You can rule out 'evening gown' right away."

Zoey refrained from pointing out that she had several swimsuits or that Benjamin himself was wearing shorts and a T-shirt. She had chosen a simple blue one-piece suit and pulled her shoulder-length blond hair into a knot on top of her head. A few stray tendrils fell down to frame her small, heart-shaped face.

"You tell me that you want to learn to surf,"

Benjamin continued. "Okay. The first lesson is: Don't spend half an hour getting ready. The second is—listen, why *do* you want to learn to surf?"

"Well . . . ," Zoey hedged. "I'm going to school in California." *I've got to stop thinking this way,* she thought. *It's disloyal to Lucas.*

"Oh." Benjamin nodded. "That makes sense. Okay, so, the first thing we're going to do is get you used to the board. Just lie flat on it and paddle a little with your arms and legs and—" He broke off, seeing her face. "What's wrong *now?*"

Zoey hesitated. "Well, it just reminds me of *Jaws.* You know how the shark looked up and saw everyone's hands and legs flailing around and it made him all hungry and—"

"Zoey," Benjamin said heavily. "*Jaws* is a movie, okay? The shark didn't look up and *see* anything. That was a cameraman. A *cameraman* saw people paddling around on a surfboard. That's it. There wasn't a real shark in the entire movie. There were only cardboard cutouts of dorsal fins and a guy in a giant rubber shark suit."

"Well, it was still kind of scary," Zoey said darkly.

"Man," Benjamin said. "You and Nina. Both—"

"Don't you dare say anything bad about

Nina!" Zoey flared. "The fact that you broke up with her doesn't give you the right—"

"I'm not going to say anything bad about her," Benjamin interrupted. "But she concentrates on the same sort of inane thing you do."

"That *was* a bad thing to say about Nina—and me, for that matter," Zoey said. "She's still my best friend, you know. Just because you've decided she's nothing but a speck of dust in your life doesn't mean—"

"That's exactly what she would say!" Benjamin said, exasperated. "She even uses that *speck of dust* expression, which is totally not true. I don't consider Nina a speck of dust. You both exaggerate things completely out of proportion."

"We do not," Zoey protested.

Benjamin began ticking things off on his free hand. "You both cry over haircuts. I don't care how bad it is; hair is not worth crying over. You both had crushes on William Shatner in the days of *Star Trek*. You both—"

"Wrong! *I* liked Mr. Spock," Zoey said quickly. "That shows how much you know."

"The point is, it's a TV show!" Benjamin said. "Mr. Spock is a TV character, not someone to have a crush on. You both ask me all the time if I think you look fat, which is such a trapdoor, I'm not even going to bother to analyze it."

"Well, all girls do those things," Zoey said calmly.

"They do not."

"Yes, they do. Name one who doesn't."

Benjamin thought. "Okay, Lara."

"I can't believe you would say something like that to me!" Zoey cried out. "You're impossible!"

"Maybe," Benjamin conceded as they reached the beach. "But I am going to attempt to teach you how to surf, and for that I deserve a Nobel Prize."

The very first words out of Christopher's mouth were wrong. He knew it the minute they were out of his mouth, but he couldn't help it. Aisha had returned a week before, and had successfully avoided him for that entire time, which was pretty amazing, given the size of the island. He was now waiting outside her house—the technical term for what he was doing was "ambush." He needed to know whether she was avoiding him, and why, although he had a pretty good guess. "Where have you been?" he asked.

He saw Aisha's shoulders stiffen. "None of your business."

Christopher decided to try again. He softened his tone. "Your mom told me that you went to Princeton."

"Then I went to Princeton. I've been back for a while, if you hadn't noticed." She brushed past him.

His impatience bubbled to the surface, but Christopher fought it down. He followed her.

"I know you didn't go to Princeton," he said.

Aisha kept walking. She had one hand on top of her head, holding up her hair. "Good for you," she said shortly.

"Kendra, uh, Kendra thought you might have gone to Boston," Christopher said carefully.

"Why would I go to Boston?" Aisha asked in a mock-innocent tone. "Why would I do that?" She turned to face him. "Why on *earth* would I?"

Man, she was making this difficult for him. "You know why."

She continued like he hadn't spoken. "I mean, I don't have any particular reason to go to Boston," she said, as though talking to herself. "Do *you* know of any reason I might go to Boston, Christopher? Is there anyone I might be interested in talking to?" She glanced at him out of the corner of her eye.

Christopher's jaw tightened. "You went to see—Carina."

"Yes, I went to see—Carina," Aisha said, imitating his pause.

"Well," he began, and then stopped.

What the hell was he supposed to say? "How is—she?"

"You sound like a robot, hesitating all the time," Aisha said. "Why don't you just say what you mean?"

Christopher took a deep breath. He had a pretty good idea of the scene Aisha had found in Boston. "Is Carina still on heroin?"

"Clearly." Aisha's sandals slapped loudly against the asphalt.

The certainty of her answer surprised him. He had thought she would say, "I guess so," or "As far as I can tell." He started to ask her how she knew, but suddenly a horrible thought occurred to him: What if Aisha had actually *seen* Carina shoot up?

A memory suddenly surfaced in his mind: Carina sitting cross-legged on the bed, leaning forward, her lips slightly parted, her huge eyes shining, a pulse in the hollow of her throat beating with eagerness, beating, beating—

Christopher shook his head. He wouldn't ask that. Besides, Carina had sometimes injected heroin, sometimes smoked it. Aisha hadn't necessarily seen her with a needle. Not that it would have been much better to see her with a pipe.

He took a breath. "Did she say anything about me?"

"Yes, she said you snore."

He was startled. "She said that?"

"No, Christopher," Aisha said wearily. "I was trying to be sarcastic, but I guess I failed."

"Oh," he said, feeling idiotic.

"She said you were great, terrific, wonderful, a real stand-up guy," Aisha said, rubbing her neck. "She said we'd be very happy together."

"Aisha, I—"

She turned to face him suddenly, and he could see the exhaustion written in every line of her face. But her eyes were glowing like coals. "Whatever lie you're getting ready to tell me—don't," she said. "Carina was, has been, and is addicted to heroin, Christopher. *Heroin.* I can't believe I had to find that out from your sister. Were you ever going to tell me about that little insignificant fact? Did it ever occur to you that it might affect my life at all?"

"Sweetheart—"

She let out a little cry, as though it physically hurt her ears to hear him call her that. She swallowed hard. "What about AIDS, Christopher? Do you have any idea what kind of risk group Carina's in? What about hepatitis, even?"

"We always had safe sex," Christopher protested. "I would never—"

"So safe that you couldn't have a baby?" The

intensity of the anger on Aisha's face was shocking to him.

He frowned. "Baby?"

"That's what I said." A tear slipped from Aisha's eye. "Baby? Small thing in diapers? Carmen? Is this ringing a bell, Christopher?"

He was stunned. "I didn't know Carina had a baby."

"Well, the baby is almost two years old," Aisha said coldly. "Go home and look at a calendar. Congratulations may be in order."

"Eesh, I haven't seen Carina for over *three* years—"

"How do I know that?" Aisha flared. "Because you tell me? Because I have your *word?*"

Christopher turned away, feeling as though Aisha had hit him in the stomach. When he turned back again, she was holding something out to him. Her engagement ring.

He put out his arm slowly, reluctantly, and she dropped the ring into his hand. Christopher watched it fall as though in slow motion, flashing in the sunlight.

She walked away and didn't even look back.

Three

2:03 P.M.

Aisha called Zoey and told her that she had broken off her engagement, causing Zoey to choke on her egg salad sandwich.

2:08 P.M.

Zoey threw the sandwich away. She called Nina and woke her up.

2:09 P.M.

Nina called Zoey back to make sure she hadn't been dreaming.

2:11 P.M.

Nina burst into Claire's room. Claire looked up from the notebook she was scribbling in and told Nina it had better be good.

2:15 P.M.

Claire called Benjamin. Benjamin said he already knew.

2:21 P.M.

Lara came over to work on the portrait of Mr. Passmore. Benjamin asked whether she had heard about Aisha yet.

2:31 P.M.

Mr. Passmore asked Lara to take an invoice over to the restaurant on her way home. Lara had to make polite conversation with Ms. Passmore for a few minutes, so naturally she dropped in the only interesting piece of news she had heard lately.

2:35 P.M.

Ms. Passmore called Sarah Mendel to ask whether she knew anything more about the situation. Sarah asked, How could she? Claire and Nina never tell her anything.

2:43 P.M.

Sarah called the Grays and asked if it was true and whether there was anything she could do. Should she bring over a cake?

2:49 P.M.

Mr. Gray hung up the phone and checked his watch.

"That must be some kind of island record," he said to Mrs. Gray.

"What *kind* of cake?" Kalif asked.

* * *

Benjamin was lying on the sofa, watching a movie on cable, when Claire came over.

"Hi," she said from the doorway. "How are you?"

"Fine," he answered automatically.

"I'll bet," she said.

Benjamin wasn't quite sure what she meant by that, so he ignored it. "Have a seat," he said instead, waving an arm vaguely. He didn't get up. His side and chest hurt. He had tried to take things easy with Zoey the week before, but it was hard to do that and still hide his injuries from his sister. So now his injuries were worse. And Zoey wanted more surfing lessons.

Claire sat on the far end of the sofa and crossed her legs. They were great legs, long and beautifully muscled, and Claire was wearing a short skirt that showed them off perfectly. Benjamin was relieved that his vision was still good enough to see them clearly.

"How's your eyesight?" Claire said, as though she could read his mind. "Is that fine, too?"

"Claire—"

"Because it wasn't last week," she said. "When we tried to catch the stalker. Or are you going to tell me that was eyestrain or night blindness or some other piece of garbage?"

"I'm going to tell you it's none of your business,"

Benjamin snapped. "I'm sorry I didn't save the day, but I was only trying to help you." Claire and Benjamin had come up with a plan to trap the stalker, which had failed at the last moment because Benjamin couldn't see clearly enough to catch him.

Claire was quiet for a moment, and Benjamin turned back to the television.

"Benjamin, look at me," Claire said, softly but firmly.

He looked at her face reluctantly. He was mildly surprised by the concern in her dark eyes.

"Tell me," she said. "Tell me what's happened to your eyes."

You can't put it much plainer than that, Benjamin thought. *And it's a good question. What* has *happened to my eyes?*

He leaned back against the couch and closed his eyes. He pressed both hands against his side to ease the pain.

"Benjamin—I'm sorry to be so blunt, but I've spent a week trying to come up with a tactful way to ask this question, and I just don't have the energy to think about it anymore. So please—"

"I'll tell you," he said quietly. "I'm just trying to remember how it began." He cleared his throat softly. "I guess—I guess it started with little things. One day I couldn't read the specials board at the restaurant. But the next day I could. And once I reached for something on the kitchen counter and knocked over two glasses. I never even knew they were there." Benjamin frowned, remembering.

"But couldn't that be nearsightedness?" Claire asked. "I mean, my dad can't even read that big two-foot *E* on the chart without his glasses—"

"No," Benjamin said abruptly. "I'm not just missing little things. Look." He pulled up his T-shirt to show her the sunburst of bruises on his chest.

Claire gasped. "Oh, my God." She leaned forward to inspect them more closely. "How did this happen? Benjamin, have you seen a doctor? You could have cracked a rib."

"All they do is tape cracked ribs," Benjamin said.

"Don't change the subject." Claire's tone became businesslike. "Does it hurt when you take a breath?"

"No, it's just sore in general," he said, watching her face. He smiled suddenly, amused at the way Claire showed her concern. It was nice that she cared.

"I'll be okay," he said, letting his T-shirt drop.

"How did it happen?" Claire demanded.

"Surfing," Benjamin said. "I never saw the wave coming."

She shook her head. "You could have—"

"I could have been hit on the head. I know. I was lucky," he said flatly. "The board just slammed me in the side."

"Oh, Benjamin." Claire let out a breath. "Is everything . . . foggy all the time?"

He shook his head. "No, some days everything's clear, but those days are rare. And—" He hesitated.

"What?" she prompted.

"Well, um, a couple of days ago I was in Weymouth, and suddenly it was like a window shade had been pulled halfway down over my left eye."

Claire looked horrified.

He smiled wryly. "It was—pretty scary," he said inadequately. "For a second I thought it was just my eyelid drooping. I stopped walking and touched my eye, but it was open. There was just this . . . this *shade* drawn over my vision, halfway down and crooked. I couldn't figure out what to do, so I sat down on a bench and closed my eyes. And I told myself: Count backward from one hundred, and then open your eyes and it'll be gone."

"Was it?"

"Not the first time I counted, but it was the second time."

Claire ran a hand through her dark hair. "What does your ophthalmologist say?"

He was silent.

She glanced at him. "Oh, God, you haven't told him, have you? How do you pull that off—have you memorized the chart or something?"

Benjamin nodded. "I tried to tell him," he said. "I even went to see him, but I chickened out. I told him that things were a little blurry sometimes. He gave me some exercises to do."

"You idiot," she moaned. "Why don't you tell him how bad it really is?"

"Why didn't you tell anyone about the stalker?" he countered.

She sighed and bit her lip. "Okay, okay," she said at last, softly. "I see your point. . . . Will you tell him if I go with you?"

Benjamin thought about it. "I don't know," he said honestly. "Because if the doctor tells me that I'm going to go blind again, I don't know if I could take it. I'd really rather not know."

"But—" Claire started, and then stopped.

Benjamin knew what she was thinking. She was thinking that maybe his vision problem was something that could be corrected. He'd had the same thought often enough. But now she was obviously following that line of thinking to its natural conclusion: What if it *wasn't* something that could be corrected?

She was silent. Benjamin understood. What was there for her to say?

"It'll be all right, Claire," he said gently, with a confidence he didn't feel. "Sooner or later I'll *have* to go to the doctor. Just let me have a little more time, okay?"

She gave him a faint smile. "Okay. I guess."

They were quiet for a moment.

"Thanks," Benjamin said.

Claire didn't ask him what he was thanking her for. She just moved closer to him on the couch.

Lucas was so tired as he tied up the fishing boat that when he heard a friendly voice say, "Can you use some help?" he looked up with a grateful smile before he even wondered who the voice belonged to.

It was Lara.

Lucas's smile faded. "Hello," he said uncertainly.

Not for the first time, he was struck by what a blend of contrasts she was, with her platinum hair and dark eyebrows, her narrow hips and full chest, her wide cheekbones and deep-set eyes. She was wearing a short gray Calvin Klein

T-shirt and faded jeans. She looked so fresh and clean and pretty that Lucas felt grimier than ever.

Lara seemed perfectly at ease. "Just tell me what I can do to help you."

Nervously Lucas directed her. "Hold these for me."

Lucas wasn't a natural fisherman, and he was a fairly new fisherman at that, and he had to concentrate as he tied the knots and fastened the lines. But even so, part of his mind was busy wondering what Lara wanted. It wasn't as though she usually went around the island offering to do good deeds.

At last the trawler was secured, and Lucas straightened up.

Lara fell into step beside him. "Headed into town?" she asked, still in that easy, companionable voice.

Lucas nodded, wondering where else he could conceivably be headed. They walked together for a few moments through the summer evening. Lucas smelled freshly mown grass and backyard barbecues. He wished with sudden fierceness that he was just an ordinary kid who could mow the lawn for a few bucks in the afternoon and then lie in a hammock in the early evening while his dad built up the fire and his mom brought out a platter of hamburgers. But instead he'd had to take over his father's fishing boat after his father died of a heart attack.

He was lost in the fantasy for several moments before he realized that Lara hadn't spoken. She was still walking beside him, though. Lucas wondered if he should be making small talk. He had never been much good at stuff like that—especially with people who made him uncomfortable. He was searching for something to say when Lara said casually, "I saw you and Nina kissing."

Lucas's foot was filled with lead. It was that simple. One second his foot had been walking along just fine, and now he had no more chance of moving it than the Tin Man in *The Wizard of Oz*—before the oil.

He and Nina had kissed. About a week ago, in the marina. It was the second time, and Lucas had sworn it would never happen again. He couldn't live with himself if it did.

He stood, frozen in place, staring at Lara, thinking, *It's over, oh, my God, she knows, she's going to tell Zoey, she might have already told Zoey, Zoey might know, Zoey probably does know right this minute, right this minute everything I care about is gone, gone, gone—*

And above this, more insistently, he was thinking: *I should have told Zoey myself.*

Lara's response was unexpected. "Relax,"

she said, and took his arm. Lucas found that his leaden feet could move after all, and he let her lead him over to a picnic table. He sat down heavily, his knees popping loudly. *I'm becoming an old man,* he thought absently.

Lara was watching him, her eyes bright and alert.

Lucas swallowed and tried to concentrate. "It wasn't—what you think," he said finally. "Nina and I are just friends."

She tilted her head. "Yes—you seemed *very* friendly."

Lucas was praying hard for some divine speaking ability. "When Zoey was in Washington, I, um, it was a hard time for me."

Lara's eyes were still on him, still watchful. *She looks like a bird,* Lucas thought distractedly. *Like a bird watching a worm.*

"A hard time," he repeated. "My father had just died, I found out I couldn't go to college, I . . ." He trailed off. Lara was looking distinctly unimpressed. He plunged ahead. "Nina had just broken up with Benjamin, she was heartbroken—"

"So naturally you turned to each other," Lara finished.

Lucas struggled to remain calm. "We—no—we . . . yes—we turned to each other. But for comfort, for friendship. That led to kissing, but it shouldn't have. Kissing wasn't what we meant to do—it was an accident."

"I see," Lara said. "An accident. Like, you slipped, and your mouth accidentally slammed into Nina's and got caught there for a few minutes?"

Lara arched an eyebrow, and Lucas knew she was remembering how their kiss looked. "I *like* Nina," he said earnestly. "That made kissing her seem natural. But I *love* Zoey."

"You can't have it both ways," Lara said.

"I know," Lucas said, exasperated. "I don't want it both ways! I just want Zoey. I'm not some creep who wants to run around on her."

"All men are creeps," Lara said, but softly, as though to herself. Her eyes were distant.

"*I'm* not," Lucas said. He spoke softly but insistently. "I want to keep Nina as a friend. But that's it. And she feels the same way."

Lara looked at her hands. "Zoey and I—haven't always gotten along," she said. "But when I saw . . . what I saw . . . I don't know, I felt sort of protective toward her. My first impulse was to tell her."

Lucas held his breath.

Lara looked up. She held his gaze, studying his eyes for something. Then she looked away.

"What's your impulse now?" Lucas asked quietly.

Lara sighed. "I know about hard times," she said. "I know all about hard times."

"I know you do," Lucas said. *Hypocrite,* he chided himself. *You never cared about what Lara was going through.*

"As long as it's over between you and Nina," Lara said, "I guess there's no reason Zoey needs to know."

Lucas tried not to let out a big relieved sigh, although secretly he felt like a death row inmate who'd just received a pardon. But at the back of his mind there was an insistent voice: *She'd never let you off that easily.*

Lucas brushed the voice aside. Lara could have already told Zoey if she wanted to. She wouldn't have sought him out if she were just going to tell Zoey everything.

"I'm glad you understand, Lara," he said.

She gave him a tiny smile.

"I'm, um, late for dinner," he said. "Should we go?" Actually, he was thinking that the longer they sat here, the greater the chance that someone would see them together, and then how would he explain that to Zoey? Zoey had a tremendous, justifiable distrust of her half sister and did everything she could to avoid her. If someone told her that Lucas and Lara were sitting on a park bench together, he would have to give her a good reason.

Lara nodded, and they stood back up.

Lucas walked along in a daze, still not quite believing that Lara knew and yet hadn't wrecked everything. Maybe luck was finally with him. Just this once.

They walked past a house on Bristol Street that Lucas had always liked. It was surrounded by a white fence, and the front yard was full of yellow forsythia. Lucas breathed in the strong fragrance, letting his constricted lungs relax. *It's going to be okay,* he told himself. *It's going to be all right.* He willed himself to believe it.

Lara was touching each newel post on the fence lightly as they passed. "So," she said brightly, "do you have any fun plans with Zoey coming up?"

M. I. T. ROOMMATE APPLICATION

Name: Claire Geiger

Age: 17

Major: Climatology

Home Address: 117 Lighthouse Road
North Harbor, ME

Race (optional):

Religion (optional): Rooster worship

Do you smoke?
Yes

If so, how many cigarettes per day?
Approximately 2 packs of menthols. More during exams.

Do you have any dorm-allowed pets? (e.g., fish, turtles)
A piranha

Do you consider yourself a "messy" or "clean" person?
Messy

Would you rather live with a "messy" or "clean" person?
Clean

In what type of environment do you study best?
Complete silence, with bare walls, in a hard-backed chair

Are you a heavy or light sleeper?

Heavy

How many hours of sleep do you typically require?

12

What are your typical waking hours?

5 p.m.–5 a.m.

How many times do you typically hit the "snooze" button on your alarm clock?

15

What type of music do you listen to?

Gregorian chants and country & western

What is your favorite television program?

I am morally opposed to television.

Do you chew gum?

Tobacco

Do you have any special dietary needs? (e.g., vegetarian)

Vegan

What do you feel is the most important characteristic in a roommate and why? (e.g., sense of humor, honesty)

Clothing size. Ideally a roommate should be one size larger than me, so that I can wear her clothes and she can't wear mine.

Do you have any medical conditions that affect your daily life?

I have sinusitis and need to sleep with the windows open a minimum of six inches year-round.

Four

Claire was rereading *Captain Jack's Self-defense* for the sixth time. She practically had it memorized.

Go for the eyes if all else fails, wrote Captain Jack. *Dig in your thumbs, and they'll pop just like two lumps of hot Jell-O.*

It took Claire a minute to identify how she felt: She was hungry. She leaned over the banister. "Janelle, do we have any Jell-O?"

Zoey found a book called *Clutter Control: Putting Your Home on a Diet* under her bed when she pulled out a suitcase. It was a library book—and four months overdue.

Aisha was reading a morbidly fascinating book called *When the Engagement Disengages.* She was halfway through chapter five: "Should You Reimburse Bridesmaids for the Dresses?"

Kate had given **Jake** a book called *The Power of Vegetarianism!* Jake was waiting patiently for his mother to lift her hamburger to her mouth so he could shout, "Wait! Don't eat that! It's alive!"

Lucas sat at the kitchen table, hunched over a paperback called *100 Ways to Save Money.*

"Don't you dare throw out that jam jar," he snapped at Kate. "We're going to make frozen-fruit juice treats."

Lara was reading a book called *Taking Your High School Equivalency Test.* She kept it hidden inside a copy of *Rolling Stone.*

Benjamin had locked himself in the bathroom and was highlighting passages out of *The Art of Attracting Women* and thinking that if Zoey or Nina ever found out about this, he was as good as dead.

Nina was just finishing a book called *Cheap Psychological Tricks: What to Do When Honest Work and Perseverance Fail.*

On the inside cover she wrote *Property of Claire Geiger* and put it in the box of books Sarah was planning to take to the church rummage sale.

Christopher squinted at a paperback edition of *How to Be a Better Communicator.* For two weeks he had been trying to come up with the words that would make everything better with Aisha. Chapter one was titled "Letting the Anger Out."

Christopher finished the chapter and carefully marked his place by folding over a corner of the page. He went into the bathroom, where Kendra was taking a shower, and cleared his throat.

"I am very angry with you for telling Aisha about Carina," he said.

Kendra poked her wet head around the curtain. "What?"

He flushed the toilet so the water would run cold. Kendra squealed. Christopher went back to the sofa and picked up his book.

Lara

Is it worth it to stay on this island for another year? I don't know.

It seems to me that everybody interesting is leaving. Like Jake. Not that he's so great—but at least he used to know how to party. And Benjamin. He's smart and easy to talk to. Somehow he knows where I'm coming from. It's probably because he used to be blind. His life hasn't been so easy, either.

At least some of the losers are leaving. Like that Aisha girl. And her Little Miss Perfect friend, Zoey Passmore. I can't wait for Zoey to get the hell off this island. Her absence is one reason to stay here. Without Zoey around gritting her teeth whenever I walk by, maybe . . . I don't know what. Maybe I'll feel differently about this whole place.

About the whole family thing. My family, I mean. Her family, too, I guess, although I just bet she wishes that weren't true. Zoey expects me to spend my life proving that I'm good enough to be part of her precious little world. Without her around acting like I'm contagious, I can get a little comfortable.

I'm sick of her attitude.

If she had to spend even one day being me instead of her, she would see just how easy it is to be so prissy when everyone has given you everything you've ever wanted for your entire life. When your whole life has been perfect.

Well, I know something she doesn't know. Zoey's world isn't so perfect.

And she can grit her teeth all she wants, but she can't make me disappear.

Five

Nina was standing in front of her dresser with a piece of Scotch tape stuck to her lower lip when Lucas appeared in the doorway of her bedroom. She blinked at him in surprise. "Hi," she said, somewhat thickly.

He smiled faintly. "Good morning."

Nina decided not to look in the mirror. It was bad enough knowing what she looked like without confirming it: She was wearing an old gray oversize T-shirt, bobby socks, and no makeup. Plus her hair was sticking up in a million places. Well, what did Lucas expect? It was eight-thirty in the morning. He was lucky she was even ambulatory.

"What are you doing?" Lucas asked, leaning against the doorjamb.

Nina removed the piece of tape from her lip and secured it on the top of her dresser. "I'm taping hairs across my dresser drawers," she said. "Because Claire is stealing my clothes."

Lucas looked skeptical.

"Look," Nina said. "I don't know *why;* I only know that she is. She claimed that her stuff and mine got mixed up in the laundry."

"I don't know very much about clothes," Lucas said. "But your clothes and Claire's are, uh, pretty different."

Nina gave him a knowing look. "Meaning hers are pretty and mine are different?"

"That's not what I meant," Lucas protested, but she just laughed.

"At any rate, if you want to make yourself useful, you can put some of this on the floor of my closet," she said. She handed him a bag of flour.

Lucas looked puzzled. "What's this for?"

"Footprints."

He smiled. "If you find one, are you going to make a plaster mold?"

Nina shook her head. "I have no faith in plaster molds after nature camp," she said. "We all spent *days* making a plaster mold of this supposed deer's hoofprint, but in the end it turned out that there was no deer. The head counselor had faked the hoofprint using this extremely disgusting deer's leg he had. It was really the end of innocence for me."

Lucas was obediently scattering flour on the closet floor. "Nina, normally I would say that maybe you have a little too much time on your hands, but I love this kind of detective thing."

Nina yanked a hair out of her head and taped it over her sock drawer. "It doesn't pay much, but it sure is glamorous. Speaking of free time, aren't you supposed to be fishing right now?"

Lucas nodded. He set down the bag of flour. "I needed to talk to you about something important."

"What?" Nina asked, her heart pounding. *Please don't say you told Zoey,* she thought. *Say anything else.*

Lucas hesitated. "Um, well, I don't know; it's probably my fault. . . . I mean . . . maybe if—"

"Just *tell* me!" Nina practically shrieked. "The suspense is killing me!"

Lucas bit his lip. "Lara saw us," he said.

He means Lara saw us kissing, Nina thought. *But he doesn't want to use that word.*

Then the full meaning of what he'd said struck her, and her legs gave way so quickly that she dropped onto a very small wooden chair that had Baby Bear carved on the backrest. Dark spots danced in front of her eyes.

"Nina!" Lucas said sharply. She felt him gripping her hands.

"I'll be okay," she said.

"You're very pale," he said doubtfully.

"I'll be okay," she said again, and he released her hands.

Her vision cleared, and she focused on him. "Has she told . . . Zoey?"

He shook his head, still looking at her worriedly. "I don't think she will, Nina. I had a long talk with her. I tried to explain that it wasn't some big hot affair."

Thanks a lot, Nina thought.

Something must have showed on her face because Lucas looked uncomfortable. "Well, you know what I mean."

Nina moaned. "Lucas, this is so terrible."

"I know, I know," he said soothingly, touching her hand again. "I've been putting off telling you because I knew you'd get upset. But we have to make the best of it. And I really don't think she's going to tell."

Nina frowned suddenly. "What's the catch?"

"What do you mean?" Lucas asked, although he looked like he knew exactly what she meant.

"You know what I mean. *Why* isn't she going to tell? It's not out of the goodness of her heart. So what's the catch?"

"Well, I wouldn't use the word *catch,* exactly—" Lucas began.

Nina covered her eyes with her hand. "Lucas, please, please, please don't get all slippery on me. Just tell me what the catch is."

She could hear him swallow. "We . . . have to be nice to her."

Nina yanked her hand away and stared at him. "We have to *what?*"

"I wonder if stalking is a full-time job," Benjamin said thoughtfully as he and Claire strolled through the tourist-filled park in Weymouth.

Claire picked a piece of lint off her linen shorts. "Why—are you planning on filling out a job application? The position's already been filled, I hate to break it to you."

"No, it's a serious question," Benjamin said, ignoring her tone. "I mean, how does this guy find the time to trail you all the time?"

Claire reconsidered. "Okay, you have a point. Not to mention the time and effort he must put into *thinking* up ways to scare me."

"Exactly," said Benjamin. "He must have a really flexible job."

"Maybe he doesn't have a job at all," Claire said.

Benjamin shook his head. "Everyone has a job."

"*You* don't," Claire pointed out. "I don't."

"That's different," Benjamin said. "We're teenagers."

They stared at each other.

A teenager? Claire thought blankly. *Some stupid teenager is doing this to me? A preteen? A kid? I've let some* kid *scare me to death?*

"Oh, my God," she said softly.

"We might be wrong," Benjamin said.

She shook her head. "No, we're right. I *know* it." She hugged her elbows in sudden happiness. "He's a *kid*."

"Claire," Benjamin said cautiously, "we really might be wrong. He could be unemployed, or work at home, or any one of a thousand things."

She wasn't listening. "Oh, Benjamin, I feel so much better!" She grabbed both his hands impulsively. "He seems so much less scary now. You have no idea. I'd been picturing this horrible man in a ski mask, and now—"

"Claire—" Benjamin tried to interrupt.

She dropped his hands and danced a few feet away. "Oh, don't talk about it anymore. I'm tired of thinking about it all the time. Listen, are you hungry?"

Benjamin considered. "I could eat."

"Well, let's go get a hot dog or something. It'll be my treat," Claire said. She dragged him toward the hot dog vendor.

"I thought you never ate hot dogs," Benjamin said, allowing himself to be pulled along. "You told me once that whenever you ate a hot dog, you woke up a pound heavier the next day."

"So I'll gain a pound," Claire said. "Come on, what'll you have?"

"One hot dog with everything," Benjamin told the vendor.

"I'll have the cheese fries," Claire said, handing over a five-dollar bill.

"Oh, you must really be feeling good," Benjamin said. "I thought you couldn't bear to look at melted cheese after that time you and Nina tried to make baked potatoes with cheese in the microwave and practically blew up the house."

"We didn't blow up the house," Claire said, accepting the cardboard container of cheese fries. "We blew up the microwave. Who knew you weren't supposed to use aluminum foil?"

Benjamin choked on a bite of his hot dog. "Who *knew?* Everyone! That's the most basic rule of microwaves. Everyone—"

"Oh, hush," Claire said good-naturedly. "I learned my lesson, okay? Nina and I were cleaning strings of cheese off the cupboards for weeks. Where should we sit? Or do you want to walk?"

"Let's walk down by the duck pond," Benjamin said. "There are fewer little kids there."

She looked at him. "Don't you like little kids?"

"Not when they keep staring at my hot dog like it's the last drop of water in the desert," he said.

Claire glanced around her and laughed.

"Okay, the duck pond, then." She ate three fries at once. "Although my fries will be all gone before we even get there."

"No kidding," Benjamin said, watching her.

Just to spite him she scooped another three fries out and put them in her mouth. But suddenly she frowned.

There was writing on the bottom of the french fry container.

*Hand*writing.

Claire swallowed the fries in her mouth and tilted the container.

"Claire?" Benjamin said.

She ignored him. She shook the remaining fries on the ground, causing a nearby group of pigeons to squawk gleefully.

"What are you doing?" Benjamin said, his voice full of concern.

Claire stared at the message written on the bottom of the french fry box. Bile rose in her throat, burning and corrosive. She fought to keep it down.

"Give that to me," Benjamin said, but instinctively Claire turned her back to him, sheltering the container with her body.

The message read: *I could get to Benjamin.*

Jake looked up as a shadow flitted across the front windows of Burger Heaven. He didn't see anything, though, so he went back to dipping fries out of the deep fryer.

Only three more weeks of this, he thought. *And then I'll go away to college, and after class I'll mosey into some diner and* order *fries instead of cook them.*

Actually Jake didn't even like fries anymore. In fact, he hated them. Whenever someone ordered them, he felt like saying, *Hey, would you like to come back and see the pit of grease we fry those in? You might change your mind.*

The shadow again. Passing the windows. Jake frowned slightly and glanced at the cash register. Max was glaring at him, and Jake realized what the shadow probably was. He leaned over the coffee machine and watched for a minute. Sure enough, Kate flashed by on a bicycle.

Jake looked at Max and shrugged apologetically. "It's my break, anyway," he said lamely. He took off his apron and walked outside.

Kate was doing a lazy figure eight in front of the diner.

"Hi, gorgeous," Jake said, trying to force a smile. She did look gorgeous. Her long red hair was tied back with a black ribbon, and she was wearing a short black dress with tiny white polka dots. But why did she have to come and hang out at his job? Ever since Kate had slipped into a clinical depression, she had become incredibly needy.

She skidded to a stop in front of him and leaned over the handlebars to kiss him.

"Hi, yourself," she said.

Jake hesitated. "Kate, Max is getting on my case again—"

"But I'm not in his stupid diner!" Kate protested. "It's a free country. He doesn't own the sidewalk."

"I know," Jake said, "but it's not like you're fooling him. He knows *why* you're riding your bike back and forth across the same eight-foot section of asphalt."

Kate sighed. "I suppose."

"Besides, it's distracting for me," Jake said, trying to lighten the mood. "I feel like I'm having an affair with Mary Poppins."

She gave him a faint smile.

"Come on, I'll see you later," Jake said.

She lingered. "I wish you could just quit this job."

"I wish I could, too," he said, fighting down impatience. "But I need the money for college."

Her face closed up, the way it always did at the mention of him leaving.

"Kate—" he started.

"See you later," she said stiffly.

He watched her pedal away, a beautiful redheaded girl out on a summer day. Why couldn't she be as uncomplicated as she looked?

* * *

Claire felt Benjamin grip her arm and spin her around. "What is it?"

She was still cupping the empty container against her, but Benjamin pried it out of her hands. He glanced at the message, tightened his grip on her arm, and started running back across the park.

Claire stumbled along next to him, her throat still scorching. *He touched those fries,* she thought sickly. *He touched the food I ate.* He was right there. *Oh, my God, where's this going to end? How much worse can it possibly get?*

They stopped in front of the hot dog cart, panting. The vendor was a sixtyish man with a bushy gray beard.

"It's a different guy," Benjamin muttered.

Of course it is, Claire thought. *I knew it would be.*

Benjamin didn't seem ready to give up so easily, though. "Excuse me," he said to the vendor. "We bought a hot dog and some french fries a few minutes ago?"

"Yeah?" The man handed a little girl a hot dog and made change from a money belt around his waist.

"Well, I don't think you were the one who sold it to us," Benjamin said. "It was someone else—your partner, maybe?"

"Oh, yeah," the vendor said. "I had to go to

the bank, so I asked some kid to mind the cart for a few minutes."

"Some kid?" Claire repeated faintly.

He glanced at her. "Sure. I do it all the time. I tell them they have to make change out of their own pockets, but when I get back, I'll give them ten dollars. It's better than leaving the cart alone."

"Do you know this kid's name?" Benjamin persisted.

"Are you kidding?" the vendor said. "I couldn't pick that kid out of a lineup. He's just a kid. Why?"

"He—he gave us a message," Benjamin said inadequately, but the vendor didn't seem to be interested. He had already turned away to deal with another customer.

Claire was cold. Goose bumps had formed on her arms and legs, and when she put her hand to her cheek, it felt like marble.

Benjamin put his arm around her and led her to a bench. "Are you okay?" He kept his arm around her as they sat down.

"Oh, Benjamin." Claire leaned her head against his chest and closed her eyes. "You heard what he said. He couldn't pick that kid out of a lineup. And neither could we. We *saw* him. We ordered from him and paid him, and I don't remember him at all."

Benjamin was quiet for a moment. "Neither do I," he said finally, reluctantly.

"He blends in *perfectly,*" Claire said. Her voice was bitter. "He might as well be invisible."

Benjamin's arm tightened around her. Claire didn't open her eyes. She didn't want to look at the bright crowded park when *he* could be anywhere, could be a few feet from them, and they wouldn't know it.

Benjamin smoothed her hair. "Well, at least we know we were right," he said. "He's a kid."

Claire said nothing. The stalker might indeed be a kid, but somehow that didn't make him any less frightening. Suddenly it made him more.

LUCAS

I should have told Zoey myself. But what would I say? "Look, Zo, while you were gone, I was really lonely and depressed and Nina and I kissed a couple of times, even though she's your best friend and all."

And Zoey would say, "That's all right; I understand." Yeah, right, just like I would if the situation was reversed.

It's too late now, anyway. Maybe if I'd gone to her right after it happened and explained it all, she would have understood. But weeks have passed . . . I've been lying to her for weeks.

I remember when Zoey was breaking up with Jake McRoyan and she kept refusing to tell him and I got so angry. I kept saying, "Why don't you just tell him?" And Z. kept saying, "Because I don't want to be the one who hurts him." I thought she was really kidding herself because obviously no matter who told him, it was Zoey who'd hurt him.

But now I have a

different take on the situation. Now I would rather have anyone else tell Zoey than do it myself. Because even though I'm the one who hurt her, it's kind of like the difference between watching someone get punched in the stomach . . . and punching them yourself.

Christopher

IN THIS COMMUNICATION BOOK I'M READING IT SAYS THAT IF YOU HAVE TROUBLE TELLING SOMEONE SOMETHING FACE-TO-FACE, OR YOU HAVE TO SAY SOMETHING DIFFICULT, OR THE PERSON DOESN'T WANT TO LISTEN, OR YOU HAVE A TENDENCY TO LOSE YOUR TEMPER, OR IT'S A SUBJECT YOU AND THE OTHER PERSON ALMOST ALWAYS QUARREL ABOUT — THEN YOU SHOULD, AS A LAST RESORT, MAKE AN AUDIO RECORDING OF WHATEVER IT IS AND GIVE IT TO THEM.

WHICH IS REALLY CORNY, AND

I WOULD NEVER DO IT IN A MILLION YEARS.

EXCEPT . . . WELL, IT'S KIND OF APPROPRIATE. I MEAN, NOTHING COULD BE MORE DIFFICULT THAN WHAT I HAVE TO TELL AISHA. AND SHE SURE AS HELL DOESN'T WANT TO LISTEN TO ME IN PERSON. AND WE'VE HAD ABOUT NINE MILLION FIGHTS ABOUT IT. AND I DO HAVE A TENDENCY (OKAY, MORE LIKE A CERTAINTY) TO LOSE MY COOL.

OH, YEAH, AND AISHA'S ENGAGEMENT RING IS SITTING ON A LITTLE DISH ON MY DRESSER AND NOT ON HER FINGER WHERE I WANT IT TO BE—IS THERE ANYTHING MORE LAST RESORT THAN THAT?

Six

Nina walked along the empty school hallway on her way to the principal's office, her clogs clattering noisily. A thin trickle of sweat ran down her back, adding to her annoyance.

In one hand she carried a folded-up letter that read:

> *Ms. Nina Geiger*
> *117 Lighthouse Road*
> *North Harbor, ME*
>
> *Dear Ms. Geiger,*
>
> *The following material(s) were not returned to Weymouth High School at the end of the spring term:*
>
> Collected Poems, by Emily Dickinson
>
> *You must either return the above item(s) or make restitution at the school office before August 29, or you will not be allowed to register for the following school year.*
>
> *Sincerely,*
>
> *Lionel Higgins*
> *Principal*
> *Weymouth High School*

In Nina's other hand was *Collected Poems,* by Emily Dickinson, which she'd found under a sweater in a corner of her room, along with an elderly ham sandwich. Nina could dimly remember throwing both the book and the sandwich there sometime last May. Still, it annoyed her to be hunted down by the school system and forced to go to the school office during the summer.

She paused for a moment outside the office. She didn't want to go in and face the school secretary, The Buzzard. Of course, her name wasn't *really* The Buzzard, but that's what everyone called her except the principal and probably Mr. Buzzard. The Buzzard would doubtless say something like, "This isn't a very good start to the new year, Nina," and sigh meaningfully.

Well, there was nothing she could do about it now. Nina took a deep breath and pushed open the door. She blinked. The Buzzard wasn't there. Instead the handsomest guy Nina had ever seen was sitting at her desk, eating a tuna fish sandwich and reading a newspaper.

He was muscular and deeply tanned, which was emphasized by the bright white T-shirt he wore. His hair was sandy and fell across his forehead, and his eyes were brown, flecked with gold. He was probably about twenty or so.

He looked up when Nina came in and gave her a smile as bright and white as his T-shirt.

"Can I help you?" he asked.

Nina had a moment of profound hindsight, in which she saw the value of picking out an outfit other than the one she had on: baggy plaid shorts and a pink blouse so old, it practically wasn't pink anymore. But it was too late now.

She cleared her throat. "I need to return this book," she said, handing him the book and the letter.

The guy took them both. "Oh, so you got one of our charming letters," he said, smiling.

Nina nodded nervously. The Buzzard's nameplate was still on the desk, but a handwritten sign taped over it read Bradley Martin.

What were they thinking, hiring him? she wondered. *Every girl in the school is going to be crowding in here.*

Brad was tapping at the computer keyboard. "There you go, Nina," he said. "All clear. Though personally I don't think anyone should be penalized for stealing a book by Emily Dickinson."

Nina smiled. "You like her?"

He nodded. "I love her. She's great." He made Emily Dickinson sound like a movie star. "What's your favorite poem?"

Nina hesitated. "The one that starts out, *Heart! We will forget him!*"

Bradley laughed. "Did you forget him?" he asked.

Nina flushed.

"You don't have to tell me," he said quickly. "Sorry I asked."

"It's okay," Nina said. "What happened to Mrs. . . ."

"Billington?" he offered.

"Yes!" she said, relieved. She would never have remembered The Buzzard's real name in a million years.

"She broke her hip and went to Vermont."

"How'd she break her hip?"

Bradley laughed again. "I like you, Nina. Not only do you read Emily Dickinson, but you're interested in all the gory details."

Nina blushed again. "I'm sorry," she said. "I guess I should have asked how she is or something."

Bradley shook his head. "No, it's a lot more interesting to talk about how she broke her hip. She was chasing the paperboy."

Nina laughed. "The way a dog chases the paperboy?"

Bradley smiled. "Maybe. But for different reasons. He'd thrown the paper in the bushes once too often, and she burst out of the house to yell at him and fell off the porch and broke her hip."

"Oh," Nina said. She was always deeply impressed by any household accident.

Before she could say anything else, Mr. Higgins, the principal, opened the door. He did a slight double take. "Hello, Nina."

"Hi," she said. She hoped Mr. Higgins wouldn't lecture her about smoking unlit cigarettes again—not in front of Bradley. She was glad she had left her trademark Lucky Strikes at home.

Mr. Higgins said, "Hello, Bradley, how's it going?"

"Just fine," Bradley said easily.

Mr. Higgins passed through the room to his own private office and shut the door.

Nina tried to think of a reason to stay and talk to Bradley, but she couldn't. "Well, bye," she said, putting her hand on the doorknob.

"Hey, Nina, wait a minute," Bradley said.

She turned back.

"How would you like a part-time job?" he said. "Working here, in the office."

"A job?"

"Yeah, we're looking for a student assistant to work second and third hours." His gold-flecked eyes watched her. "It pays peanuts, but it might be fun."

He thinks it might be fun to work with me! Nina thought joyfully.

Bradley smiled coaxingly. "You'd get out of two whole classes," he said.

Nina knew as well as the next person that only the biggest nerds and stool pigeons ever worked in the school office. It would ruin her image as Unbelievably Sexy Woman of Mystery. It would terminate any chance she would ever have at a social life. She didn't hesitate.

"I'd love to," she said.

Ever since she'd broken off her engagement, something strange had happened to Aisha's family.

For example, they no longer shouted her name irritatingly from the foot of the stairs. They no longer banged on the wall if she played her CDs too loudly. They no longer barged into her room without knocking. Now if they needed her, they would tiptoe down the hall and tap on her door with the gentlest of rappings, even if her door was open.

They no longer woke her every morning at 6 A.M. Now they let her sleep as late as she liked. Only since Aisha wasn't sleeping very well, it would be more accurate to say that they let her lie in bed as long as she liked. And when she did appear around ten or eleven, her mother no longer said, "Well, good *morning,*" in that sarcastic way that used to drive Aisha crazy. Instead her mother would quickly set aside whatever she was doing and come closer—but not too close—to Aisha and say, "How did you sleep? Would you like some breakfast?"

They no longer complained about her finicky appetite. Her father no longer grumbled that they weren't running a restaurant—or rather, they *were* running a restaurant, just not one that catered to picky teenage girls. Now Aisha found that her favorite dishes, sometimes two or three of them at once, were always served for dinner.

Her parents no longer pretended they couldn't hear the bickering between her and Kalif. They no longer said that they had more important things to do than settle disputes between children who were too ill-mannered and immature to behave civilly. Just the opposite—now if they so much as heard Kalif say, "Hey, I was watching that!" her parents sped into the living room, wrestled the remote control out of Kalif's grubby fist, and handed it sweetly to Aisha. Then they gave Kalif such a stern look that he would hang his head in a way that almost broke Aisha's heart.

Strangest of all, they didn't want her to work. They wouldn't *let* her work. If Aisha picked up a guest's breakfast tray or a laundry basket, her mother would take it from her and thrust it into the hands of Kendra or a very startled Kalif. "Don't you worry about *that,*" her mother would say. "You go—"

And then her mother would pause and bite her lip because really, where could Aisha go? Over to Zoey's, who would treat her just as oddly? Nina's? Over to *Christopher's?*

So Aisha packed for college. She sewed name tags in all her clothes. She folded the clothes neatly and packed them in boxes along with her books and CDs and photographs and posters and blankets. She filled eleven boxes, taped them shut, and labeled them. Then she cleaned out her closet and desk drawers and covered her bedroom furniture with dust sheets.

Her room looked like it couldn't wait for her to leave, to go off and live in some other room, which was kind of depressing, so Aisha stopped hanging out in her room. She went for walks.

She didn't want to run into anyone she knew, so she took the ferry over to Weymouth and walked for hours through the streets there. She window-shopped and saw tons of things she would like to buy. Unfortunately she didn't have very much money. That was one thing that hadn't changed. Her dad still said, "Aisha, I'm not made of money," although sometimes after he said it, he got a kind of stricken expression, as though he'd just remembered who he was talking to.

Aisha wanted these walks to tire her out so she could sleep, but they didn't. No matter how many hours she walked, she still lay awake in bed at night, thinking of Christopher and how much she wanted to hate him.

She supposed that the reason the walks didn't tire her out was because, back before her family became so strange, her mother used to make her run up and down the stairs a million times a day, and as a result the muscles in Aisha's legs were like iron.

She was thinking about this one day as she walked along the Weymouth main street and she happened to look up and see a sign that read:

Weymouth Mini-triathlon
August 21
Amateurs Only
First Prize: $500
See community center for
details and registration

Aisha flexed her steely legs and went in search of the community center.

Jake frowned when he saw the envelope addressed to "Jane McRoyan" in big loopy handwriting lying on the floor under the mail slot. He ripped it open and began reading.

Dear Jane, the letter began. *Hi! My name is Miranda, and we're going to be roommates. I'm seventeen, blond, blue eyed, five-seven, and really into sports.*

Jake checked the envelope again. Yes, it was clearly his address. He went back to the letter.

Do you like to ski or play tennis? Those are my two favorites, but I also like biking, hiking, golf, squash, soccer, and jogging. Pretty much anything . . .

There was more, but Jake didn't read it. He pulled a piece of paper out of his mother's desk and wrote quickly:

Dear Miranda,

Nothing would make me happier than to be your roommate, but I'm afraid there's been some sort of mix-up. My name is Jake, not Jane, and I'll be living in the guys' dorm. Besides, I have a girlfriend.

However, you sound like a really great person and maybe we can still meet sometime.

Sincerely,

Jake McRoyan

He mailed the letter on his way to work and didn't bother to wonder why no one from the guys' dorm had written.

Seven

Christopher settled himself in front of his stereo with a glass of iced tea. He inserted an empty cassette into the tape deck and pressed record. "Testing . . . one, two, three."

He stopped, rewound, and played the tape. "Testing . . . one, two, three." His voice sounded tinny and nasal.

Christopher rewound the tape again, cleared his throat about twenty times, pressed record, and began talking:

Eesh, uh, I called you today, and your dad said you had a message for me, which was that you had joined the foreign legion. And, uh, since I'm pretty sure you didn't join the foreign legion, I guess that means you're still not talking to me.

I know that you're confused about Carina and . . . things, and this book I read said that sometimes it's easier to explain yourself on a tape—

Christopher broke off, considering. He decided there wasn't any real need to tell Aisha that it wasn't his own personal gesture. He rewound the tape a little.

I know that you're confused about Carina, and you deserve an explanation. But since you won't speak to me in person, I decided to make this tape for you.

He paused to take a sip of his iced tea.

Okay . . . I met Carina in high school. I was walking into school one day through the back door, where all the smokers hung out, and this bunch of girls were just stubbing out their cigarettes and going in, too, so I held open the door for them. Most of them sort of snorted at me, but the last girl in the group said thank you and gave me a shy smile. That was Carina.

I saw her again the same day after school, sitting on the tailgate of someone's truck, and she smiled again. She was wearing this T-shirt with a rainbow on the front and she was so tiny that she looked a lot younger than she was and . . . well, she didn't look like a junkie then. I don't know how she looked when you saw her in Boston, but when I met her, she just looked like a pretty girl. We started going out. We dated for six months.

Carina was on heroin already by then, but I didn't know it. We never went to parties because we didn't have any friends in common, so I didn't get the chance to see her in action. And she never showed that side of herself to me. Never. Once I saw her at McDonald's late one night with a group of people I didn't know, and she was so stoned, she didn't even recognize me. At the time, I was just upset by the fact that she was out with someone other than me. I was really, really jealous, not worried over how stoned she was. She apologized the next day and said that they were some friends of her sister's and that she'd just had too much to drink and smoked a little pot, and we made up.

So, um, after about six months Carina left home. She told me that it was because her father was abusing her, but later I wondered if maybe her father had found out about the heroin. . . . I don't know. Carina didn't, uh, she didn't have a very good home situation, so it could have been abuse, I guess.

Anyway, she began crashing at friends' houses, and after a while she dropped out of school and got this lousy job working the graveyard shift at a 7-Eleven, which she said she needed because she was paying her friend's parents' rent. I couldn't stand to see her like that, and everyone knows that the graveyard shift is the most dangerous one as far as robberies go, and I kept thinking about her there alone and every night, and . . . I, uh, asked her to marry me.

My mom pretty much flew off the handle and said that I was throwing my life away, but I didn't see it like that. I mean, I thought the situation wasn't ideal, *but I loved Carina and I didn't see that we had much choice. We got married despite my mom's objections, and Carina quit her job. My mom relented a little and said we could live with her for a bit while we tried to find our own place.*

Carina was as good as gold while we lived with my mom, although she didn't go back to school. She said they wouldn't let her until the new term started. I found out later that was another lie, but . . . anyway, neither my mom nor Kendra noticed anything suspicious while Carina lived with us. I didn't have time to notice anything. I was too busy going to school, coming home and looking at apartments with Carina, working part-time as a bag boy at the supermarket, and then doing my homework just before I went to bed.

Finally we found this rattrap of an apartment that we could afford, and we moved in. Right away we began fighting. Carina said she was bored being home all day. I wasn't very sympathetic to that particular complaint since I was so tired that one night I actually fell asleep standing up in line to cash my paycheck. Anyway, I told Carina to get a job if she was so bored, and she went back to the 7-Eleven, where they put her on a short morning shift this time.

She stopped complaining about being bored then, but things didn't get any better. We still fought like crazy, and I began noticing that she could never account for her time. Like I would say, "What did you do today?" and she couldn't think of one single thing. And she couldn't account for her money, either.

And then one day, it was a Saturday, I came home from work early to see her. Usually I had to work Saturday nights until midnight—that was another thing that caused stress, but we needed the money. Anyway, that night my boss offered to let me go early if I came in for an unscheduled shift the next day, and I jumped at the chance. But when I got home, Carina seemed really surprised to see me and not in an altogether good way. I made dinner, and in the middle of it she suddenly said she knew of a party she really wanted to go to and asked me if I would go with her.

I said, "What party?" and she said some girls from school had come into the store and invited her. That sounded reasonable, and I thought going out might be good for us, for both of us, so I said okay.

Christopher's throat was dry. He stopped and took a drink of tea. His eyes were far away.

So we got to the party, and two things were immediately clear. One, that it was a drug party. Two, that Carina had been here before. Everyone knew her by name, and a couple of people even knew me. "Oh, yeah, Christopher,*" they said. "The husband."*

Carina parked me on a couch and disappeared. I sat there, thinking. I thought about how Carina never had any money. I thought about how she was never home when I called in the afternoons. I remembered this bruise I'd seen on the inside of her elbow and how she said it was from moving boxes at work.

But it was just like the other time, the time I saw her at McDonald's. I was jealous more than anything else. I didn't stop to think that what she was doing was dangerous, or illegal, or possibly fatal. I just worried about who *she was doing it with, and how often she came to parties without me, and what she did when I wasn't here. I remember looking at every guy in the room and wanting to punch their lights out.*

About this time Carina came back.

Christopher stopped talking. There was no sound other than the scratching of the tape. He was silent for perhaps thirty seconds.

I can still see how she looked that night perfectly. She was wearing a white blouse, and she had a pendant that I'd given her on a white ribbon around her neck, and her hair was this heavy curtain of tiny curls and waves. . . . She looked like an angel. She crossed the room and knelt beside me. She took my hand and held it against her cheek and said, "Christopher, I want you to do something. I want you to do something with me. Will you?"

I nodded. I would have done anything for her at that moment, anything.

She smiled and kissed me. She took me by the hand and led me to one of the back bedrooms. She knocked on the door, and someone said, "Who is it?" and she said, "Me, Carrie." I remember thinking that I'd never heard anyone call her Carrie before, and then we went inside.

A girl and a guy were sitting on the bed. The guy was obviously pretty stoned, but the girl seemed okay, or at least sober or straight, whatever. She said, "Hi, Carrie," in a bored way and gave me a hard look.

"This is Christopher," Carina said. She

sounded happy and proud, like she was introducing me to someone at a class reunion. "He's okay."

Looking back, I guess okay *meant I wasn't a cop. At the time I didn't know what she was talking about. Anyway, the girl didn't seem very convinced, but she gave me another hard look and said, "You know the rule—guests go first."*

Carina said, "Yes, yes," in this eager way and sort of pushed me over to the bed. I sat down, and she sat down next to me. Right away started searching through her purse for something, and pulled out a small pipe. She stopped when she saw me watching and gave me a smile. "It's okay," she said gently.

"Carrie," the girl said impatiently, and Carina sort of giggled and said, "Oh, here, here," and handed the girl some money. The girl rummaged around in the drawer of a nightstand and handed Carina a bag full of a sticky black substance—I couldn't tell what it was, although I had a pretty good guess.

I watched as Carina's dark eyes became at ease and happy, and when I looked up, the girl had turned her face to me. "You ready?" she said.

I looked at this girl, this girl who looked so untrustworthy that I wouldn't want her to be my waitress, and I thought, Are you crazy?*—and then I saw Carina.*

She was leaning forward, watching me, and her eyes were shining. She was looking at the bag. Then she raised her eyes and smiled at me, a bright hot smile.

Christopher paused. When he continued, his voice was thick.

I told the girl I was ready. . . .

Eight

Christopher handed Kendra a cassette. "Give that to Aisha when you see her tomorrow morning," he said. "And don't screw up."

I think I can manage, Kendra thought with more than a little irritation. She slid the cassette into her purse and promptly forgot all about it.

Lucas was sitting on the Passmores' couch, watching MTV with Zoey's feet resting in his lap. Nina was sprawled out on the floor in front of them, eating popcorn the way a cat drinks milk—with her tongue.

Zoey was wearing some ridiculous navy blue play skirt, and normally Lucas would have been mesmerized by the idea of touching her tanned thigh right where the hem of the skirt touched it, but tonight he was too busy waiting for something disastrous to happen. He was fairly sure it would. He had been lucky for over a week now, but he knew that his luck was sure to run out.

Zoey reached out with one of her feet and wrapped her toes around a lock of his hair. "You need a haircut," she said.

Nina was watching from the floor. "What are you, a monkey?" she said to Zoey.

Zoey's toes released the lock of hair. "What do you mean?"

Lucas caught her foot. "She means the way you use your toes to pick things up."

Zoey flexed her other foot, considering.

Nina stared. "Oh, my God, your toes are as long as my fingers."

Zoey sat up straighter. "My toes are *not* as long as your fingers."

Nina held her hand against Zoey's foot. "They practically are. I bet you could peel a banana with your toes."

Lucas expected Zoey to be offended, but she merely looked intrigued. "Maybe . . ."

"A banana sounds good," said Lucas, who was hungry.

Both girls laughed. "I'll go get one—" Zoey said, half rising. "Oh, wait, I want to watch this video. I like this song."

They fell silent, watching Hanson.

"You know," Lucas said thoughtfully. "Those girls would be pretty if they didn't look so much like boys."

Zoey and Nina stared at him for a minute

and then burst out laughing. "They're *brothers!*" Nina said.

"Are they?" Lucas said, studying the screen. "I thought—I thought it was just Swedish fashion sense or something."

"Swedish!" Nina shouted.

"They're from Oklahoma!" Zoey said, laughing. "How could you think they were girls?"

"Well, they're wearing ski sweaters," Lucas protested. Both girls laughed even harder at this.

"Look," he said, trying to defend himself. "I thought they were some Swedish girls with husky voices. Look at their hair, for God's sake."

Zoey rolled off the couch and clutched Nina. Nina was laughing so hard, she had tears in her eyes.

"Stop!" Zoey begged. "If you say anything else, I won't be able to breathe."

Lucas was about to say that *Hanson* was a brand of ski boot, when what he had been fearing all along happened.

Lara appeared in the doorway of the family room, a puzzled smile on her face. "Hi," she said. "What's so funny?"

Zoey was suddenly conscious of the fact that her skirt had ridden up, and she smoothed it down.

"Nothing's funny," she said to Lara. "I mean, nothing we can really explain." She knew she sounded rude and sullen and childish, but she couldn't help it. Lara seemed to bring that out in her.

"Oh," Lara said comfortably. "An inside joke." She set her purse on the table by the doorway. She was wearing white shorts and a deep blue denim shirt. It made her pale hair glow.

"Benjamin's not here," Zoey said shortly.

"I know," Lara said. "He has photography class tonight."

Zoey nodded. She wanted to say, *If you knew that, why'd you come over?* But she didn't. She couldn't be *that* rude. She dropped her eyes and began idly picking fluff out of the carpet.

"So," Lara said, looking at the three of them. "Are you guys going to watch a movie?"

Zoey looked up sharply. How did Lara know that?

"No," she started to say, but Lucas interrupted her.

"Actually we were thinking of watching *The Stepfather,*" he said.

Zoey twisted her head around to look at him in annoyance. Why was he volunteering information? Let Lara get whatever she came for and leave. Lucas didn't meet her eyes, and his next sentence was even more amazing.

"Have you seen it?"

What's he doing? Zoey thought frantically. *That's practically an invitation.*

"It's scary," Nina said. She sounded—shy. Nina shy? "We were waiting for it to get completely dark."

"I like scary movies," Lara said.

Well, who cares if you do? Zoey thought. *Because we're not inviting you to watch with us.*

But it almost sounded as if that's exactly what Lucas and Nina *were* doing.

"The first time Claire and I watched it, we screamed all the way through," Nina continued in that timid, un-Nina-like way. "And, like, two *days* later one of our neighbors said, *Are you girls okay? I heard all kinds of screams.* Which was a little late, you know? I mean, two days had gone by."

"Where is the video, anyway?" Lucas said. "Is it in the VCR already?"

Zoey had the wild desire to clap and say, *Time out! Has everyone gone crazy?* Why were Lucas and Nina being so—so nice? On second thought Zoey didn't care why. She just knew that she wasn't going to sit around and watch a video with Lara. She'd rather leave her own house if it came to that. In fact, that's just what she would do.

Zoey stood up. She waited expectantly for Nina to scramble to her feet also and for Lucas to rise from the couch. They would make up something, some excuse about needing something from Nina's house, a forgotten dentist appointment, an overdue library book, *anything*.

But neither Lucas nor Nina budged. Lucas rummaged under the sofa cushions for the remote, and Nina said, "Would you like some popcorn, Lara?"

Lara shook her head and sat on the edge of an armchair.

"Let me get the lights," Lucas said, stretching to hit the switch.

The room went dark, Nina settled herself more comfortably on the floor, and finally—feeling confused and betrayed—Zoey sat back down.

Nine

Kate walked slowly back from Jake's. He'd been packing for college, and that depressed her. Why couldn't they just lie down and hold each other until he had to leave? Why did he have to leave at all?

She shook her head, knowing she was being ridiculous. Jake was dying to go to college, just like everyone else. Kate would love to go back, too—if only she were well enough.

I'm crowding Jake, she thought miserably. *I can see it in his face. It drives him crazy. But why can't he understand that right now I really need someone to lean on? Someone with rock solid feelings about me?*

She walked with her head down, so lost in thought that she jumped when a voice said, "Hello, Kate."

She looked up and almost gasped.

Her mother was sitting on the Cabrals' doorstep.

Kate had never seen her mother sitting on a

doorstep before. She had never seen her mother sitting on anything except the most comfortable chair in the room, whichever room they happened to be in. Usually with a glass of white wine in one hand, the other wrist absently shaking the gold bangles she always wore.

"Hello, Mother," she said at last.

She expected her mother to stand up immediately and dust off the back of her pale rose-colored suit. But her mother remained sitting. "I got your letter, Kate," she said at last. She picked a rhododendron off the bush by the porch and held it to her nose.

Kate didn't know what to say. She'd hoped never to see her mother again when she wrote that letter. She'd made it clear that her mother didn't understand her, or her depression, and that her presence was unwelcome—to put it mildly.

"It was quite a letter," her mother said.

Kate cleared her throat. "Yes," she said. "It was."

Kate's mother still seemed preoccupied with her flower. She felt the petals with her fingertip. "Perhaps we could talk," she said.

Kate was surprised. Her mother never started sentences with *perhaps.* Most of her sentences started with *I.*

Her mother apparently saw the surprise on her face because she smiled wryly. "What do you say we go over to Portland and find a decent restaurant?"

Kate thought about it. "No," she said finally. "If you want to talk to me, you're going to have to do it here."

Lara smiled to herself when Zoey jumped to her feet as soon as the movie was over. Zoey was obviously chafing at her presence.

"Lucas, I'll walk you home," Zoey said firmly. "I know you have to get up early. I'll be right back, Nina."

She stressed the last word, and Lara knew that Zoey meant for Nina to stick around so they could have some dumb gabfest or braid each other's hair or whatever the hell it was they did.

Zoey obviously also meant for Lara to leave because she said, "Good-bye, Lara," in that same firm voice.

"Good-bye," Lara said in her most gracious voice, leaning back in the easy chair and crossing her legs. She saw Zoey's lips tighten in annoyance.

"Come on, Lucas," Zoey murmured.

"'Night," Lucas said uncomfortably.

Lara smiled faintly at him as he and Zoey left.

Nina was picking stray pieces of popcorn off the carpet and throwing them into the bowl. "Well," she said, dusting her hands off. "I guess I'd better get going."

"Aren't you going to wait for Zoey?" Lara asked.

Nina lowered her eyes. "No . . . I have stuff to do tomorrow."

I'll bet you and Zoey don't have so much to talk about these days, do you? Lara thought.

"What do you have to do tomorrow?" she pursued.

Nina looked taken aback. "Oh, just . . . back to school nonsense," she said. She cleared her throat. "What, um, what are you up to?"

Lucas told her, Lara thought. *Lucas told her I know. She's dying to leave, but she's afraid to be rude to me.*

"No plans yet," Lara said, shrugging.

She picked up her purse, and Nina carried the bowl of popcorn into the kitchen. Benjamin was just coming in the door.

"Hey," he said with genuine pleasure. "You guys aren't leaving, are you?"

"Sorry," Nina said stiffly. "Don't eat that; it has carpet fluff in it," she added as Benjamin grabbed a handful of popcorn.

"A little carpet fluff never hurt anyone," Benjamin said. "Don't you want to stay? I have some new prints from class."

"Good *night,*" Nina said to Benjamin, trying to edge past Lara.

"Good night, Nina," Lara said, deliberately lingering.

Nina's eyes flashed, but she only said, "See you."

She doesn't like me staying with Benjamin, Lara thought.

"Want a Coke or something?" Benjamin asked as the door closed behind Nina.

"No, I'd better be going, too," Lara said regretfully. She would have liked to stay and talk to Benjamin, but she was afraid he would ask too many questions about what she was doing here. "Maybe tomorrow?"

"Sure," Benjamin said easily.

Lara went out the door and down the walk. She could see Nina just disappearing around the corner. She wondered what Benjamin would think of Nina if he knew about Nina and Lucas. Wouldn't he be disappointed in her? Would he be jealous? What would he think—

Lara froze as a new, terrible thought occurred to her: *What would he think of Lara if he found out she was a blackmailer?*

Suddenly Lara didn't want Benjamin ever to know. She would do anything to keep him from finding out, even if it meant relinquishing the wonderful power over Zoey. Tomorrow she would go to Lucas and tell him not to worry, that she was sorry if she'd made him uncomfortable, that she didn't blame him—she'd tell him anything. But Benjamin must never, ever know.

Lara's heart was beating rapidly, and she felt a

little panicky. Maybe she should go find Lucas *now.* Maybe—

A flash of pale color caught her eye. It was Zoey's hair, catching the moonlight as she walked back from Lucas's house. She was walking dreamily up the road, obviously having just had some big good-night make-out session with Lucas.

Zoey walked with her arms crossed and her hands cupping her elbows. Something about her posture drove Lara crazy. It looked like she was hugging herself. It was so—so *smug.* Irritation bubbled up inside her, and she swept aside her vow of the minute before. Getting even with Zoey was worth any price, even Benjamin.

"Good night, Zoey," Lara called, happy to see Zoey look up from her reverie, startled. Lara waved. "See you soon," she added.

Ten

Kalif looked at the stopwatch. "Ready . . . set . . . go!"

Aisha took off running backward up the stairs, her knees jerking like pistons.

Kalif started laughing and dropped the stopwatch.

Aisha stopped. "What?" she asked, annoyed.

"I didn't know you were going to run *backward,*" Kalif said, holding his stomach. "You look like a chicken."

"I do *not* look like a chicken," said Aisha, who privately thought she probably did. "Now quit laughing and time me."

Kalif sighed. "Okay," he said, clicking the stopwatch. "But why are you running backward?"

"Because it's a good way to strengthen my calves," Aisha said, coming back down the stairs. "It's also a good way to have a heart attack."

"Is that why you're wearing a pacemaker?"

"It's not a pacemaker; it's a heart rate monitor," Aisha explained impatiently. "Now will you get ready to time me, please?"

"All right," Kalif said. He held up the watch. "Ready . . . set . . . go!"

Aisha took off again. This time she was halfway up when her mother appeared at the bottom of the stairs. "Aisha!" she called. "What on earth are you doing?"

Aisha stopped again and rolled her eyes. "Training, Mom."

"Well, you're making a horrible racket," Mrs. Gray said. "The guests will complain."

"I've been doing it all morning and nobody's complained yet," Aisha said.

"You've been doing it all morning!" Mrs. Gray repeated. "I thought that was Kalif carrying the laundry upstairs." She turned to him. "Have you done that yet?"

"I'm timing Aisha," Kalif said.

"Well, stop timing her and start carrying," Mrs. Gray said. "Aisha, go train somewhere else."

"But Mom, I'm *supposed* to run up the stairs backward," Aisha protested. "The triathlon guidelines recommend it."

"Why backward?" Mrs. Gray asked. "You look like a chicken."

"Mom!" Aisha said.

Kalif laughed.

Mrs. Gray ignored him. "Aisha, we happen to live at the top of a very steep hill. I'm sure it'll be just as rigorous training if you go run backward up that," she said. "Lunch is at one."

Aisha sighed and gathered up her stopwatch and water bottle. She grabbed a towel and walked out the front door, patting her neck dry. She was wearing gray athletic shorts and a white tank top, which was practically transparent with perspiration. Her sports bra felt like a wet straitjacket.

The mini-triathlon consisted of three parts: a one-mile swim, a ten-mile bike race, and a two-mile run. Because the cycling part and the running part came right after each other, it was called a "brick." The guidelines didn't say *why* it was called a brick, but Aisha thought it was probably because that's what your legs felt like when you were trying to run the last part.

She trudged down Climbing Way and set her towel and the stopwatch on the ground. She couldn't time herself, anyway. She took a drink of water and checked her heart rate monitor: one hundred thirty-six. According to the triathlon guidelines, you were supposed to check your heart rate at various times and fill it into the following formula:

> Working heart rate = maximum heart rate – minimum heart rate x % effort + minimum heart rate

The problem was that even when Aisha wasn't busy working out, she was so busy thinking bad things about Christopher that her heart rate was pretty much sky-high all the time.

Aisha shrugged. She wasn't too sure about the percentage of effort, anyway, so the formula probably wouldn't do her much good.

She took a deep breath and began running backward up the hill. She jerked up her knees. *Hup!* she thought with each step. *Hup! One! Hup! Two! Hup! Three! Hup!—*

"Ooof!" Aisha grunted as she collided with someone.

"Ouch!" the person said as he fell.

Aisha fell on top of him, her hip landing solidly in his stomach.

"Oh, my God, I'm so sorry," she said, scrambling to her feet. "Let me—" She broke off.

The person lying on the ground was Christopher.

It had been weeks since she had actually spoken to him, and her eyes ran hungrily over his face. Then her anger took over.

"Why don't you watch where you're going?" she snapped.

Christopher got to his feet slowly, rubbing his abdomen. "That's ironic, coming from someone who was running backward," he said.

Aisha supposed this was true, but she didn't want to concede anything. "What are you doing here, anyway?"

"I was bringing a book to Kalif," Christopher said, still holding a hand to his stomach.

"Well, you can give it to him when I'm gone," Aisha said shortly. "Or you can mail it to him. But right now you can just turn around and go straight back home."

"Aisha—" he started.

"Just go," she said firmly.

He stayed for a moment, studying her in a watchful, wary way. "Did you at least listen to it?" he asked.

Listen to what? Aisha thought distractedly. *What's he talking about now?* But she was too angry to ask.

"Go on," she said, and actually stamped her foot at him, as though he were a stray dog she was trying to scare away from the garbage and not somebody she loved.

Used to love.

"Are you watching?" Zoey called.

Lucas nodded, thinking that probably every guy on the beach was watching Zoey in that wet suit. The only people Lucas had ever seen wearing wet suits before were dumb-looking surfer guys with so many thigh muscles they walked bowlegged. The look on Zoey was completely different—and fantastic.

He watched Zoey carefully sit on the surfboard

and begin paddling out. He had already taken out the boat and done the first check of the lobster pots, and he would have to go out again in an hour. He couldn't really afford the time or fuel to come back in between, but how many more days would he be able to spend any time with Zoey at all?

Besides, it was worth it, just to stand in the sand with the sun warming his skin and the smell of suntan lotion and saltwater and fresh air filling his nostrils—and not the smell of fish.

A very small wave approached Zoey, and Lucas watched her turn her back to the wave and start paddling toward shore.

Don't forget to watch the wave, he told her silently.

As if she heard him, she glanced behind her and angled the board slightly away from the peak, insofar as such an extremely small wave could be said to have a peak. She sneaked a quick look at him, and he smiled encouragingly.

Zoey began to stand, lost her balance, then tried again. This time she pushed herself into a very shaky standing position. She carefully placed one foot in front of the other.

Hurry, Lucas thought. *That wave could be halfway back across the Atlantic by now.*

But the little wave seemed to be cooperating with Zoey, rolling slowly, keeping its small peak and catching the surfboard gently. Zoey must have felt the board accelerate because she leaned into the wave and then—she was surfing!

Lucas wanted to jump up and down and cheer.

She was riding the wave, all right, her legs shaky, her arms overbalancing a little, but all in all pretty good. She rode the wave in to about ten yards from shore, when it flattened out beneath her.

Sit down, Lucas thought.

"I did it!" Zoey screamed. "Oh, did you see?" And then the board tilted and she slid off its slippery surface.

She popped up a moment later, laughing and pushing her hair out of her face. She splashed into shore and threw her arms around Lucas. "Did you see?"

"Oh, yes," he said. "I was—hey!" He broke off in surprise as Zoey jumped totally off the ground and wrapped her legs around his waist.

"Aren't you proud of me?" Zoey asked, dripping water all over him. "Though I guess I'm proud enough of myself."

"Very proud," Lucas said, giving her a squeeze.

She kissed him saltily, hungrily, and Lucas tightened his grip on her. "Mmmm," Zoey said, breaking his kiss. Suddenly her eyes widened. "Oh, wait, I'd better get the board. If it floats away, Benjamin will kill me."

Lucas released her, and she dropped lightly

to the sand. She ran down and rescued the surfboard from the tide and carried it back up shore. "Do you have time for lunch?"

"Sure, if it's a quick one," he said. He'd actually been planning on swinging by the Grays' house. He'd bumped into Kendra down at the marina and she'd asked him to give a tape to Aisha, explaining that she was supposed to do it yesterday, but today was her day off and she didn't want to go near the B&B for fear of being put to work. But Lucas wanted to have lunch with Zoey. Aisha could wait for her tape. She could survive without Boyz II Men or whoever for a few days.

"Well, I brought some stuff from the restaurant," Zoey said, spreading out a towel. "It's in the paper bag."

Lucas sat next to her on the towel and helped her unpack containers of cold rice, cold noodles, cold green beans. Everything in the Passmores' refrigerator was always one day old and cold—and delicious.

He glanced over at Zoey, who was eating a cold stalk of broccoli, and smiled. He pushed a lock of her wet hair behind her ear. "You want to do something tonight?"

She looked at him out of the corner of her eye. "Sure . . . as long as it's us, and not us and Lara."

Lucas had just taken a bite of chicken. At the

word *Lara* his throat closed, and he wondered how he would be able to swallow.

"What came over you the other night?" Zoey asked. "You and Nina both! You were both being so—*nice.*"

"Come on, Zo," Lucas said thickly, trying to sound normal. "You've said before that we can't be rude to her or your dad will get on our case."

"There's a difference between rude and *nice,*" Zoey said. "Can't we stick to ignoring her?"

"Well, Benjamin likes her," Lucas said.

"So let *Benjamin* hang out with her!" Zoey said, exasperated. "Look, you know how I feel about her—and I certainly don't want to spend my last few weeks on the island with someone who is rude and selfish and—"

"Okay, okay," Lucas said soothingly. He ran his hand down Zoey's side. "You look great in that suit."

She gave him a knowing look. "Don't try to change the subject." Suddenly she laughed. "All right, go ahead and change the subject, especially if you want to pay me compliments."

Lucas smiled. "You surf well, too."

"Benjamin is not going to believe it," Zoey said. "You should have seen him the first day he tried to teach me, shouting and beating his hands against his leg. It was like being coached by an orangutan."

Lucas finished his chicken leg. The mention of Lara had sufficiently destroyed his appetite. "Want to try again?" he asked Zoey. "Then we'll have a quick swim, and then I have to go."

"Oh, okay," Zoey said, picking the last few noodles out of a container with her fingers.

She grabbed the board and ran a few feet into the water. Then she stopped and smiled at him over her shoulder.

Lucas tried to freeze that moment in his brain. He tried to stop the drops of water as they glittered in the air around her; he tried to memorize the way Zoey's wet hair fell across her cheek, the sweetness of her smile.

Later he found that he could always remember the way she looked at that moment.

Claire

11:01. Cold front moving in from the east. Storm predicted. God, I hope so.

Aaron called last night from some noisy bar, and we're talking, and all of a sudden he says, like he just remembered, "Are you still getting crank calls?" and I said "Yes." So Aaron asks, "Any more notes?"

He calls them notes, like they're something someone passed me at recess. I call them—well, never mind what I call them.

I said, "Yes, more notes"

(although he didn't catch my ironic tone), and then I told him about what happened with Benjamin in the park.

So all Aaron has to say is, "What were you doing with Benjamin?" What a jerk! First of all, he's off probably screwing half of America, and he's jealous because I go to the park with my ex-boyfriend? And what about the fact that the stalker threatened Benjamin? What if something happens? Did Aaron think of that? No! He wants to know what I'm doing in the park with Benjamin.

I swear, sometimes I wonder if I even know him at all.

Eleven

Benjamin finished writing the lunch menu on the restaurant specials board and rubbed his hands against his jeans. He hated the dry feeling of chalk. He surveyed the board, wishing his handwriting were better.

He walked across the empty restaurant to the far wall to see if he could read the board from there. He squinted a tiny bit. Yes, there it was, all legible. His eyes must be having a good day. Without even realizing what he was doing, he put his hand over his left eye.

"Benjamin," his mother interrupted mildly from the corner table where she was adding receipts, "it's a specials board, not an optical illusion."

"I know," he said, embarrassed. "I just want to make sure it's intelligible."

Ms. Passmore seemed about to say something else when the door opened and Lara hurried in, her face flushed and her arms full of books. "I'm sorry," she said nervously, looking from Benjamin to his mother. "I know you're not open yet, but it's about to rain and I have all these library books. . . ."

Ms. Passmore smiled. "We don't have to be open for you to come in, Lara. I'm glad you thought of us."

Benjamin silently blessed his mother. He loved her for being so gracious and forgiving after everything Lara had put them through. Not to mention that Lara's mere existence was evidence of their father's affair—she was a live painful memory for Ms. Passmore.

"Is it raining?" he asked. The shades were still pulled on the windows, and he couldn't see out.

Just then the sound of rain hitting the windows startled all three of them.

"These summer storms . . . ," Ms. Passmore said. "You got here just in time, Lara."

Lara took a napkin from the dispenser and carefully dried the cover of the top book in her pile. "I don't think they got too wet," she said. "Do they, like, examine them when you return them or what? I never had a library card before."

Benjamin and his mother were both quiet for a minute. Benjamin assumed it was because they were both having the same startled thought: *You never had a library card before?*

He cleared his throat. "No, they don't examine them," he said. "They expect a little wear and tear."

"What books did you get?" Ms. Passmore asked.

Lara suddenly looked nervous. "Oh, nothing much; I—"

"Hi, Lara," Mr. Passmore said, coming out of the kitchen with an apron tied around his waist over a tie-dyed shirt. "Did you come in to wait out the storm? Want something to eat?"

"Oh, no, thanks," Lara said.

At that moment everything went dim, and Benjamin's heart nearly stopped. He could only see the vaguest shapes, the faint glow of Lara's T-shirt.

Oh, my God, he thought. *It's happened why didn't I see the doctor oh God not again I can't go back—*

"Jesus, the electricity," he heard his father say.

"Do we have any candles, Jeff?" Ms. Passmore asked.

"Do you really think we need them? It's the middle of the day." Mr. Passmore sounded doubtful.

"Jeff." Ms. Passmore laughed. "I can hardly see you!"

"I'll get some from the back."

A power outage. Benjamin felt weak. He groped for the nearest chair and sat down heavily. His heart was pounding, and his skin felt clammy and cold. He pinched the bridge of his nose and breathed deeply.

After a moment Mr. Passmore came back, lighting his way with a lit candle. He dumped the rest on the table in front of Benjamin. Benjamin lit one with shaking hands.

Ms. Passmore was struggling into an old rain slicker. She slipped a candle into her pocket. "Guys, I'm going up to the house to make sure all the windows are closed. I should be back before the lunch crowd. Will the food be okay, Jeff?"

"Sure," Mr. Passmore said, still lighting candles. "The generator should kick on in ten minutes. Nothing will spoil that quickly. Power will come on at the house then, too."

"Okay, then," Ms. Passmore said. "Bye, everyone."

She left, and Mr. Passmore finished lighting candles and putting them in holders. Benjamin rubbed the back of his neck. He felt a little better.

"Okay," Mr. Passmore said. "Both of you take a couple of candles and come into the kitchen. We're going to have our first pasta lesson."

"Now?" Lara said.

"Yup," Mr. Passmore said. "You're going to make linguini with pesto sauce, and if it's good, we'll eat it for lunch and if it's bad, we'll put it on the specials board."

Lara and Benjamin exchanged a smile and a shrug. They each picked up a candle and followed Mr. Passmore into the kitchen. As he walked past the table where Lara had been sitting, Benjamin glanced at the pile of library books. The top one was titled *Remedial Math*.

The kitchen had no windows, and the door was shut against the storm, but the candles made it bright and cozy.

"Okay, this'll be like a cooking show," Mr. Passmore said. "You guys are the celebrity guests, and I'm the host. Lara, you can grate the cheese. Benjamin, start chopping up the basil leaves."

They worked while Mr. Passmore started the water boiling on the gas range. "Pesto is very important," he said. "Not many people can do a good pesto—shoot, I don't have enough linguini here. I'll get some from the storeroom."

As he left the room Benjamin smiled at Lara. "He's loving this," he said softly. "I think he's trying to impress you."

"Impress me?" Lara looked surprised.

"Yes, because, you know, you're such a talented artist."

"Oh . . ." Lara shrugged. "That's nothing."

"I would give anything to draw like you do," Benjamin said honestly.

"I would—I would give anything to be going off to college," Lara said.

Benjamin wanted to ask her more, ask her about the library books, but just then Mr. Passmore bustled back into the kitchen.

He surveyed their progress. "Okay, everything into the bowl. Lara, you begin whisking lightly."

Benjamin heard a faint humming. "Is that the generator?"

"Should be," Mr. Passmore said absently. "That's probably mixed enough."

Lara held the bowl closer to the candle. "I hate to break it to you, but no one's going to eat this."

"Why not?"

"Because it looks like pea soup, for one thing," Lara said.

"I was thinking it looked more like baby food myself," Benjamin said.

"Don't be silly," Mr. Passmore said. "It's Zoey's favorite."

That was the wrong thing to say. Even in the candlelight Benjamin saw Lara's face turn sullen.

The overhead lights came on, flickered, steadied. The kitchen suddenly seemed sterile. Mr. Passmore opened the back door. "The storm's over," he said. Benjamin could see weak sunshine outside.

He glanced back at Lara's face, thinking that everything should seem brighter and happier now that the sun was out, but somehow it didn't.

Twelve

Lara was eating macaroni and cheese and wishing that she could afford cable. Instead her only entertainment was sliding the pieces of macaroni onto the tines of her fork and eating them four at a time. She was getting tired of macaroni and cheese, but it was cheap, so she ate a lot of it.

She was just wishing that she knew what Lucas and Zoey were doing that night when her doorbell rang. Lara was startled. Her doorbell never rang. She hid the bowl of macaroni in the wastebasket and went to answer.

It was Mr. Passmore, with a big Tupperware bowl in his hands.

"Hi, Lara," he said with his big goofy grin. "Are you busy?"

"Hi," Lara said. "Um, no, I'm not busy at all. Come on in."

Mr. Passmore held out the bowl. "Actually I come bearing gifts. I made gazpacho at the restaurant, and no one at home will eat it, but *I* love it. Do you like gazpacho?"

"I don't even know what it is," Lara said.

"It's a kind of cold spicy tomato soup," Mr. Passmore said.

Well, gross, Lara thought. *No wonder no one likes it. Thanks a lot for coming over and trying to pawn it off on me.*

Mr. Passmore was looking at her eagerly. "Do you want to try some? Or have you had dinner already?"

"I'd love to try it," Lara said. "Have a seat; I'll get some bowls."

Mr. Passmore sat at the kitchen table while Lara found a couple of presentable dishes and furtively washed them. She poured them each a glass of water while Mr. Passmore dished out the gazpacho from his Tupperware bowl and even produced a little plastic bag of crackers from his pocket. Lara shook her head. What a nut.

She sat down and tasted a spoonful.

"Well, what do you think?" Mr. Passmore asked, looking like a million dollars rested on her answer.

She smiled. "I love it," she said, although privately she thought it would taste better hot.

Mr. Passmore smiled delightedly. "I knew you'd have better sense than those knuckleheads," he said. He winked at her. "You must take after me."

Lara stared at him. He almost never referred

to any family resemblance or father-daughter tendencies. She lowered her eyes.

Eating dinner with Mr. Passmore was easy because you didn't have to worry about making conversation. He ate with a kind of animal contentment and only rarely broke off to say something like, "Isn't this the best gazpacho?" or beans or turkey or whatever you happened to be having. He ate five bowls of gazpacho in a kind of dreamy state. Lara ate two.

"Oh, that was great," Mr. Passmore said, sitting back in his chair.

Lara smiled at him with genuine fondness. "That was really good," she said. "Thanks for bringing it over—uh—thanks."

She had been about to call him "Mr. Passmore" when she remembered that he wanted her to call him Jeff. But she didn't know if she could bring herself to do that yet. She'd only recently stopped mentally referring to him as "Zoey's father."

"It was a pleasure, Lara," Mr. Passmore said, not seeming to notice her awkwardness. "When are you coming over to work on the portrait some more?"

"Oh, I don't know," Lara said, caught off guard. "Whenever you like. Or—or we could do some now if you . . . don't have to get going."

"Really, you can do it here?" Mr. Passmore said. He didn't look at his watch or show any signs of leaving. "Don't you need the same background?"

She laughed. "No, I put the background in last, anyway. Let me do a little sketching."

She walked into her bedroom and got her canvas and easel. She didn't feel like getting out all the oils, but she could do a little work with charcoal. She was having trouble with Mr. Passmore's eyes.

She lugged the easel back into the kitchen and started setting it up. "This'll be—"

"Lara—" Mr. Passmore interrupted. His voice was subdued.

She looked up. He was holding a piece of yellow paper in his hands.

Lara swore silently. It was the eviction notice from her landlord. She'd stuck it in her napkin holder and forgotten all about it. It was a month old already.

"Lara," Mr. Passmore said. "This is serious."

"I know," Lara said. "But I fell behind in the rent and . . ." She trailed off.

"How many months do you owe?" Mr. Passmore asked quietly.

"Three," Lara said miserably.

"I see." Mr. Passmore let out a long breath. "Lara, you have to let me help you."

Lara bristled. "How? Are you going to pay for an apartment for me the same year that both Benjamin and Zoey start college? You're going to support four separate households? Is that it?"

Mr. Passmore grimaced. "I see your point, Lara. You don't have to attack me. But I can't let you get evicted, either. Zoey and Benjamin have financial aid. I can probably manage something." He tapped the eviction notice thoughtfully against his chin. "What about . . . what about if you moved in with us, with Darla and me?"

"Darla and you—and Benjamin and Zoey."

"They're leaving for college in a couple of days. You know that."

Lara hesitated. She wondered if maybe Mr. Passmore finding the notice had been a blessing after all. "Where—where would I stay?"

"In the garage apartment—"

She shook her head immediately. "No, thanks. I'd appreciate it if you'll lend me whatever you can afford to help me with the back rent, but—"

Mr. Passmore looked puzzled. "What's wrong with the garage apartment?"

"I lived there before," Lara said, crossing her arms, "and I always felt like the family pet, living in the *garage*."

"Lara, it wasn't like that."

"It *was*," she insisted. "Remember what you said when you got here? You said, *Do you like gazpacho? No one* at home *does*."

Mr. Passmore looked pained. "I said that? I only meant—"

"I know what you meant," Lara said. "But that's the way it was when I lived in the garage apartment. It'd be even worse now."

"But . . ." Mr. Passmore paused, deep in thought.

Lara waited for the idea to occur to him. When it did, she could see it as clearly as if it were written on his forehead.

"Well, what about if you took Zoey's room?" he said.

"Really?" Lara said. She leaned forward and put her hand on his arm. "You'd let me stay in Zoey's room? Do you think she'd mind? Don't you need to check with her first?"

Mr. Passmore looked a bit uncomfortable at the mention of checking with Zoey, but he only smiled faintly and said, "Of course not. It's not like she'll be using it while she's at college. She couldn't possibly refuse. When can you move in?"

"Whenever," Lara said, gesturing at the notice. "Probably the sooner the better."

"Well, Zoey has a trundle bed," Mr. Passmore said absently.

Lara took her hand away from his arm. "My rent is due on the twentieth of the month. How about then?" she said. She stood up quickly to clear their plates before Mr. Passmore could see the gleam of triumph in her eyes.

Thirteen

"Claire, you've been looking so thin lately," Burke Geiger said, examining her from across their booth in Pizza Hut. Claire and Nina had met him there after an afternoon of shopping. "You should eat more."

Claire gave him a slight smile. *Of course I'm thin,* she thought. *I'm scared to death most of the time. It really kills my appetite, no pun intended.*

"Well, then, let's have double cheese and pepperoni," she said lightly.

"Nobody's ever said that to me," Nina said. "Nobody has ever, ever said, *Nina, you're too thin—have another cookie.*"

"You're just right," Burke said reassuringly. He looked at both girls fondly. "Just think, this is probably the last time I can meet the two of you for dinner. Soon—"

"Dad," Nina interrupted. "I literally feel sick to my stomach every time you say, *It'll be just Nina and me.* Do you have to keep reminding me?"

"Nina—"

"Anyway," Nina continued. "As much as you and I might wish it, Claire's not going away permanently."

"I'm not even going that far away," Claire added.

"Yes," Nina said, nodding. "Not far enough, by any means—"

"Okay, girls," Burke said hastily. "Tell me what you've been up to this afternoon. Shopping?"

"Yeah," Nina said, rummaging in her bag. "Oh, shoot, Lucas gave me this tape to give to Aisha and I completely forgot. . . . Anyway, I bought a Luscious Jackson CD."

Burke looked puzzled. "A what?"

"I bought some clothes," Claire intervened quickly so they wouldn't have to spend an hour translating.

"Well, good, then maybe you'll stop wearing mine," Nina said.

"I'm not wearing your clothes," Claire lied. She'd been buying clothes ever since her entire wardrobe had been slashed, but she still needed to use a few of Nina's. Otherwise she'd be wearing the same thing every other day. She'd been trying to be subtle and mix them up.

"You are, too," Nina said, gesturing at Claire's body. Claire was wearing a brand-new T-shirt and an ancient black "skort" kind of thing. Nina couldn't have worn it in years.

Claire wondered how she recognized it.

"Dad—" Claire began, but Nina cut her off.

"So if those aren't my clothes, why do you look like someone who got dressed as they ran out of a burning building?"

"Look," Claire said, annoyed, "if they're your clothes, don't be so critical. You're always telling us it's high fashion."

"That was a trap!" Nina shouted triumphantly. "I knew if I insulted you, you'd admit that was my skort!"

"I said *if*," Claire shot back. "I said *if* they were your clothes—"

"Girls, girls," Burke said. "Please. Maybe it's a good thing there's only going to be one of you for a while after all."

"Well, it's true, Dad," Nina said moodily, slumping farther into her corner of the booth and licking the butter off a piece of garlic bread. "She's been wearing my clothes. They all smell like Obsession."

"Speaking of smells," Burke said hastily. "Has either of you been smoking in my car? It smells like cigarettes."

Oh, my God, Claire thought sickly.

"Dad," Nina said, pulling a Lucky Strike from behind her ear and holding it out to him. "In case you haven't caught on yet, these are *un*lighted."

"Well, I'm just asking," Burke said. "Maybe one of you had a friend who—Claire, are you okay? You look queasy."

Claire put a hand to her face. "It's the garlic bread," she said shakily. "It's a little buttery for me." She stood up. "I think I'll just get some air. I'll be back in a second."

Burke rose from his seat, but she put a hand on his shoulder. "Don't worry." She walked quickly out of the restaurant to her father's silver BMW.

Slowly she approached the driver's-side door and unlocked it. She slid behind the wheel and gently closed the door.

Claire leaned her head back against the headrest and inhaled. The smell was very faint, but her father was right. The car did smell like smoke.

It's just kids, she told herself, resting her fingertips against the padded steering wheel. *Just kids fooling around, sitting in a BMW, smoking. It's not necessarily* him.

She pulled open the ashtray. A single cigarette butt lay at the bottom. Claire hesitated, then picked it up. Marlboro. *Great, only the most common brand in America,* she thought. *Great clue.*

But did it matter how common the brand was since it was only kids? Of course it didn't matter. Then why did Claire have such a persistent image of—of *him,* sitting in her father's car, carefully, methodically smoking one cigarette?

He would have made a game of it, she thought. *He would have said to himself, I'll just smoke one cigarette, and if he shows up before then—*

She shook her head. How could he have thought any of those things when it wasn't him? When, for the last time, *it was just kids,* or maybe Nina and some dumb friends of hers.

She opened the door and got out, feeling better. As she swung the door shut something in the backseat caught her eye. Claire stared at it through the window. It was her father's raincoat. Burke always kept it thrown carelessly in the backseat. Claire stared at it.

Go back inside, a voice in her mind thought.

But Claire didn't go back inside. Slowly she swung the door back open and leaned across the bucket seat to reach for the raincoat. She held it open between her hands.

Claire had seen this raincoat so many times over so many years—or else one just like it; Burke's style never varied—that for a few seconds she didn't see what was in front of her. Her brain almost succeeded in superimposing a memory of the raincoat over the one in her hands.

Claire blinked, and the image vanished. This raincoat was slashed to ribbons.

"Go!" Kalif shouted, and Aisha dove into the Pressmans' pool and swam five laps.

She surfaced and spit out some pool water. "Well?" she asked Kalif, blinking.

He studied the stopwatch. "Two minutes and five seconds."

Aisha calculated mentally. Five laps of the Pressmans' pool was exactly one twenty-fourth of a mile, so two minutes, five seconds, multiplied by twenty-four . . . Fifty minutes! She groaned.

"What?" Kalif asked. "Isn't that good? You were going pretty fast."

Aisha hauled herself up the ladder. "I'm hoping to do a thirty-five-minute mile," she said.

"A thirty-five-minute *mile?*" Kalif repeated. "A mile? I could do it faster on a *tricycle.*"

Aisha had very little doubt that he could, but she decided not to waste time explaining that water is one thousand times denser than air or about water drag and percentages of efficiency. Instead she stood on the edge of the pool and said, "Let me try it again."

The Pressmans' sliding glass door opened, and Mrs. Pressman stepped out with a cordless phone in her hand. She said, "Phone!" at exactly the same moment that Kalif screamed, "Go!"

Half of Aisha's mind heard Mrs. Pressman and reached for the phone. The other half heard Kalif and tried to dive. The end result was that she fell into the pool with one arm stretched out.

She surfaced and climbed the ladder

sheepishly. Kalif was laughing, and even Mrs. Pressman was smirking.

"Thank you," Aisha said to Mrs. Pressman, taking the offered phone. She wondered who was calling her here. She didn't care as long as it wasn't Christopher.

"Hello?"

"Aisha?" A male voice. But it wasn't Christopher's. Aisha felt a pang of—disappointment? *No,* she told herself sternly.

"Aisha?" the voice asked again.

"Yes?"

"This is Graham Stevenson."

"Who?"

"Graham Stevenson. We met on the bus? Going to Boston?"

"Oh, yeah," Aisha said, not caring if she sounded rude. That bus ride had been a million years ago, back when she still held out hope for herself and Christopher.

"Well," Graham continued, sounding a little uncertain. "I called your house, and your mom gave me this number."

"Yes?"

"I, uh . . ." Graham cleared his throat. "It's just that one of my professors asked me if I could recommend a teaching assistant, and I thought of you—"

"Well, thanks, but I'm going to Princeton," Aisha said.

"You didn't sound completely certain when we talked," Graham said.

That was because I thought there might be some reason to be closer to home, Aisha thought. *I know better now.*

"I'm certain now," she said firmly. "Thank you for calling me. Good-bye." She pushed the off button on the phone and handed it back to Mrs. Pressman. "Thanks."

"Oh, it's no problem, Aisha," Mrs. Pressman said. She acted as weird as Aisha's family these days. She had actually called up and offered Aisha the use of her pool for training purposes and even cleared her kids out of the way. There were some advantages to being publicly heartbroken. "Why don't you stay and swim a little longer?"

"That would be wonderful," Aisha said gratefully.

"But I want to go home and watch *Beavis and Butt-head,*" Kalif protested.

"Well, go," Aisha told him. "Although that's a really mindless show." *Christopher likes it, too,* she thought. *That* proves *it's mindless.*

Kalif went inside with Mrs. Pressman, and they closed the door behind them. Aisha dove into the pool and swam more laps.

She was still marveling at Graham's call. *He must have remembered my name and looked me up in directory information,* she thought. *Just what*

I need, another stupid man *meddling in my life.*

She was glad she'd told him no, but she still thought longingly about the teaching assistant job. Graham hadn't even said what subject. Chemistry? Astronomy? What did a teaching assistant actually do?

Aisha floated on her back, staring at a few early stars. Her body was exhausted and completely relaxed now from the water. She would sleep well tonight—she hoped.

The sliding glass door opened again.

"Oh, I'm just getting out," Aisha called. She swam to the shallow end and walked up the steps, water streaming off her. "Thanks again—"

She stopped. Christopher was standing in the square of light reflected from the house. He closed the door behind him.

"What are you doing here?" Aisha demanded furiously, snatching off her swimming cap. Even if she wasn't engaged to Christopher anymore, she still didn't want him to see her looking like Humpty Dumpty.

"I'm here to clean the Pressmans' pool," Christopher said. Aisha saw that he was in fact holding a pool skimmer.

She crossed her arms. "Oh, and you just *happen* to come to clean the pool while I just *happen* to be here?"

"Yup," Christopher said.

Aisha felt stupid. Maybe it was just a coincidence. "Well, in that case," she said lamely, wondering what case she was referring to, "I'm leaving."

"Fine," Christopher said.

Aisha glared at him. He could at least act *interested,* damn him. This was Christopher, after all. Didn't he even want to look at her newly muscled body in the wet swimsuit?

She stalked over to the Pressmans' picnic table, pulled her T-shirt roughly over her head, and stepped into her shorts, feeling a big wet spot appear on the seat of them. She didn't care.

She grabbed her bag to stuff her swimming cap into it but dropped the bag. "*Damn* it," she whispered angrily, kneeling to retrieve her keys and wallet and Walkman.

She stood up and found Christopher looking at her intently. Actually he was looking at her Walkman intently.

"What—what are you listening to?" he asked, a high strange note in his voice.

Aisha stared at him incredulously. They had recently become disengaged, and Christopher wanted to make small talk about what kind of music she liked?

She pushed past him, hopped briefly on one foot to pull on her sandals, and walked to the glass door. It was locked.

Aisha knocked. She could feel Christopher's eyes on her back. She knocked again. She would climb the fence in a minute or else burst a blood vessel.

She heard a strange beeping sound. She knocked again. Where *were* the Pressmans? The beeping didn't stop. Aisha looked down. It was her heart rate monitor.

She ripped it off and threw it against the cement floor, where it clattered and then went quiet. Aisha could only imagine what the beeping meant. How fast did your heart beat when it was breaking?

Ms. Claire Geiger
117 Lighthouse Road
North Harbor, ME

MIT Residence and Campus Activities
104 Hamden Hall
Cambridge, Massachusetts

Dear Ms. Geiger,

Thank you for completing and returning your roommate application. After careful consideration, we feel you would be happiest in a single room and have assigned you to 603 Barron Hall.

Please complete and return the enclosed housing card by August 24. . . .

Fourteen

Zoey squeezed Lucas's hand as they boarded the ferry. "Look, the whole gang's here, practically." She waved to Nina and Aisha. Nina was sitting near the railing, watching Aisha as she jogged in place.

Every time Zoey thought about leaving for California, a wave of nostalgia swept over her. All the normal everyday things she had done a million times before seemed so precious, like riding on the ferry. *It's just like it was last May,* she thought as they crossed the deck. *If only Benjamin were here. And Claire.*

Good God, Zoey thought, startled. *Did I just wish for Claire?*

A touch Zoey could have done *without* was stupid Lara, sitting farther down the railing, reading a book. *Reading a book?* Zoey thought distractedly.

"Hey, I always thought the ferry was powered by engines, but now I learn it's Aisha," Lucas said. "Are there twenty more girls jogging in place down below?"

Aisha gave him a scornful look. She stopped running and took her pulse, counting off the seconds on her watch.

"Seriously," Lucas said. "You can buy a heart rate monitor, you know."

Aisha gave him an even more scornful look—Zoey wasn't sure why—and said, "Aren't you supposed to be fishing?"

"I need a part for the boat," Lucas said. "Zoey's keeping me company." He put his arm around her shoulders and pulled her in front of him, his chin resting on top of her head. Zoey leaned against him happily. She would miss him so much. . . .

"Where are you going, Eesh?" Zoey asked.

"To the high school to use the track," Aisha said, touching her toes.

"You're awfully quiet, Nina," Lucas said.

"I'm busy trying to think of something I'd want to do less than enter a triathlon," Nina said. She paused, then added, "I can't, in case you were wondering."

"You're all going to be jealous when I win five hundred dollars," Aisha said. She held her ankle and pulled her foot above her head.

"Yes, but we're not going to be jealous when you end up in traction," Nina said, watching.

Aisha lowered her leg. "And where are you going, Nina?"

Nina looked cagey all of a sudden. "Um, to my job," she said.

"Job?" Zoey asked.

"Yeah, I work at the, um, the school office."

There was a moment of silence.

"You're kidding," Lucas said.

Nina looked annoyed. "Why would I be kidding?"

"Because only the biggest dorks ever work in the office," Lucas said. "The Buzzard handpicks them."

Nina lifted her chin. "Listen, I get out of second and third periods," she said defensively. "And if I don't like it, I can always quit."

"Uh-uh," Aisha said. "They make you sign some nerdball contract. I know from student council."

All this time Zoey had been trying to figure out what looked different about Nina, and now she had. Nina was wearing eye shadow. Zoey studied the rest of Nina. She was wearing a kelly green sleeveless suede vest and faded jeans. She looked pretty, really pretty. But why was she so dressed up to go and assist old Buzzard?

Zoey was just about to ask this when the ferry lurched into the landing. "Oh, shoot," she said. "We barely got to talk at all. And we *never* see you anymore," she said to Aisha. "Do you want to do something tomorrow?"

"Well." Aisha considered. "I'm supposed to go cycling. You guys could come with me."

"Okay," Zoey said. *Aisha needs us right now,* she thought. *The least we can do is go for a bike ride.*

"Actually I'd like that," Lucas said. "I could get home at four."

"Nina?" Zoey said, giving Nina the evil eye.

"Love to," Nina said weakly.

"Cycling?" asked a soft voice.

Zoey turned. Lara had joined them, her book tucked under her arm. "You guys are going for a bike ride this evening?"

Zoey sighed loudly and looked away. Not even Lara could fail to be dismissed by a gesture like that.

She almost jumped when she heard Lucas say, "Um, do you want to come, Lara? I have an extra bike."

Zoey stared at Lucas, her blond eyebrows drawn together in consternation.

Lucas smiled at her, but there was something weird about his smile. Something *dry.* It seemed to Zoey that she could actually see his upper lip sticking to his teeth.

He smiled at her again, stopped, ran a hand through his hair, and stared out at the water, his Adam's apple jutting out as he swallowed.

* * *

Nina crunched the handle down on the binder, praying that it would go all the way through this time. She checked the sheaf of papers. Oh, thank God. She slid the binding on carefully. It was her twenty-fifth copy of Mr. Carmine's required reading articles for American history. She had 125 more to go, and her arm already felt like a noodle.

There was a knock on the supply-room door, and Bradley poked his head in. He had a three-ring notebook under his arm. "How's it going? Do you need a little break?"

Nina smiled at him. "I'd love a break."

Bradley was even more handsome than she had remembered from the previous week. She liked the angularity of his face and the brightness of his smile. She liked the way his gold sweatshirt brought out the gold flecks in his eyes. She liked everything about him, basically.

"How's your arm?" Bradley asked. "That machine is murder."

Bradley looked pretty muscular, and Nina doubted that it was murder on *his* arm, but it was still nice of him to say so. She flexed her arm. "I feel like I've just milked an entire herd of cows," she said, "with one arm tied behind my back."

Bradley laughed. "Here, let me rub it for you." He picked up her wrist with one hand and ran his other hand up her arm and began kneading the muscle gently. "Feel better?"

"Mmmm," Nina said. She didn't trust herself to say anything more. Bradley's touch was warm and tingly. Nina was suddenly deeply thankful that she'd worn something sleeveless.

"So, do you know a guy named Donald Huckman?" Bradley asked.

Nina tried to concentrate. "Um, yeah, he fixed our grandfather clock once."

Bradley's eyes sparkled. "Yes, he seems like the kind of guy who fixes people's grandfather clocks in his spare time. Anyway, he just came by, wondering if we were looking for a student assistant."

"He actually came in and asked that?"

"Oh, yes, and he was very disappointed that the job was already taken." Bradley's fingers were still warm on Nina's skin. "He's going to be the substitute."

"Oh . . . good," Nina said vaguely. She was looking at Bradley and thinking that she would probably never miss another day of school in her life.

"So, speaking of this job," Bradley said, and to her disappointment dropped Nina's arm. "Mr. Higgins wants you to take a look at this." He tapped the notebook he'd brought in with him.

Nina glanced at the cover: *Student Assistant Job Reference Book.*

"Do you mind if I look through it with you?" Bradley asked.

"Oh, no, not at all," Nina said.

Bradley pulled a chair up next to hers and leaned close. *How on earth am I going to concentrate?* Nina wondered. His arm was touching hers.

She opened the notebook. The first page was a list of all the previous student assistants. Nina knew most of them in person or by reputation. They were the biggest geeks in high school.

I'm not going to be too thrilled to see my name in that lineup, she thought. She brushed the thought aside. Bradley was worth it.

She turned the page. Student Assistant Job Agreement, it read at the top. This was the "nerd-ball" contract Aisha had warned her about.

Nina began reading:

1. I promise to arrive promptly for my shift.
2. I promise not to make personal calls on my shift.
3. I promise not to have friends visit me at my desk.

Nina looked at Bradley. "I really, really don't think number three is going to be a problem," she said.

He laughed.

4. I promise not to do homework at my desk.
5. I promise not to steal school supplies.
6. I promise not to write letters on the Weymouth High School letterhead.

"Oh, now see, I never would have thought of that," Bradley said, pointing to number six. "But once they suggest it, it's pretty tempting."

"Well, look at number seven," Nina said. "Talk about tempting."

7. I promise never to look through the principal's or the secretary's desk drawers.

"Yeah, what do you think they're hiding?" Bradley said. His eyes were just inches from Nina's own. She looked away.

8. I promise to always give the substitute at least two hours' notice.
9. I promise to work from September 1 to May 30, excepting school holidays.

Then there was a place for Nina's signature and the date.

"Well?" Bradley asked. "What do you think?"

She risked another look at him. He was so close, so handsome.

Nina signed the contract with a flourish.

"Congratulations," Bradley said. He blew on the ink to dry it. She watched his mouth. "The rest of the book is pointers from previous student assistants," he said.

"That's hilarious." Nina laughed.

"I know," Bradley said. "Let's read them."

They put their heads together over the book, and Nina thought: *He's so much like me. He loves to mock things. He doesn't take himself seriously. He's—*

Suddenly the door to the back room opened, and The Buzzard stood there on crutches.

Nina gaped at her.

"For heaven's sake," The Buzzard snapped. "The front desk is completely deserted."

"I'm sorry, Mrs. Billington," Bradley said, rising. "This is Nina Geiger—she's going to be the student assistant this year."

"I'm well aware of who she is," The Buzzard said, giving Nina the once-over. "As for being my student assistant, I can see that the interview process for that position has completely deteriorated. Have you read and signed the contract?"

"Yes, ma'am," Nina said weakly.

"Good, because I intend to hold you to it," The Buzzard said crisply.

Nina frowned. What was The Buzzard talking about? And why wasn't she in Vermont? Perhaps she had just come back to help whip the place in shape before the school year.

The Buzzard turned back to Bradley. "Well, don't just stand there; get back out to the front desk before somebody walks off with the whole place. Don't think you can slack off just because it's your last day."

A ringing sensation filled Nina's head. "Last day?" she whispered.

Both Bradley and The Buzzard turned to look at her.

"Did you say something, Nina?" The Buzzard said. "For heaven's sake, speak up."

Nina cleared her throat. "I said, this is Bradley's last day?"

Bradley nodded. "I go back to school in two weeks. I'm taking some time off to go backpacking."

"School?" Nina croaked.

"Yes," he said with a smile. "I go to the University of Montana."

"You do?" She dragged her eyes to The Buzzard's face. "You—don't you live in Vermont?"

"I have a summer house there," The Buzzard snapped. "Not that it's any of your business. Get me a cup of coffee, Nina. I'm not supposed to be on my feet."

Nina didn't answer. She was suddenly sure that there was a cartoon balloon above her head. She was almost certain that if she put her hand up there, she would feel it—light, fluffy, cottony. In it would be written one word in very large letters: *Zonk!*

Fifteen

Claire was so exhausted that she could barely lift her soup. Every spoonful of chicken noodle soup that touched her lips seemed like an individual miracle.

"Is the soup okay, Claire?" Janelle asked worriedly from the doorway.

Everyone turned to look at Claire.

Claire forced a smile. "Oh, yes, it's delicious."

She hadn't slept in days.

Not since she had found her father's slashed raincoat. She had stayed awake until she was sure her father and Sarah were asleep, and then she'd sneaked out to the BMW and retrieved it. It was now buried at the bottom of her closet along with all her other slashed clothes.

But even after that, she couldn't sleep. She was too frightened. She couldn't protect her family all the time. Her father was often alone in the ferry parking lot, Nina was alone in the yard, Sarah was alone in the house, Janelle walked home after dark. . . . They were all in danger. All because of Claire. She squeezed her eyes shut against the images of their defenselessness.

"Claire, are you okay?"

She opened her eyes. Burke was looking at her with concern.

"Just sleepy," she said, giving him a real smile. She'd made up some excuse to take the ferry in with him early that morning and then convinced him to come home for lunch. But she couldn't follow him around all the time.

"So where was everyone when the power went out?" Burke asked.

"I was in the basement doing laundry," Sarah said, "when it went pitch-dark. I could barely find the stairs."

Thank God that wasn't me, Claire thought. *Being alone in a dark basement would probably have polished me off. Just being in my room was bad enough.*

"I had just plugged in my curling iron," Nina said. "I thought I'd caused it."

Claire gave her an irritable look. "How could you cause a blackout by plugging in a curling iron?"

"Well, it's a very big curling iron," Nina said. "And what with the timing and all."

"Didn't you notice that there was a *storm* going on?"

"Look, I only thought it for a *second,*" Nina said. "I admit it wasn't a brilliant hypothesis.

Why don't you go take a nap if you're so tired? You're really cranky."

"Me?" Claire said. "You're the one who came home and slammed the front door. Did you have a hard day at the *office?*"

"What office?" Burke asked.

"She has a nerdy job at the school office," Claire said. "God knows why."

Burke's face lit up. "Nina, I think that's wonderful—"

"Dad, just stop right there," Nina said, pointing her spoon at him. "I don't want to hear it. If you want to help, you can have one of your corporate lawyers look into releasing me from a contract. Otherwise pipe down."

"Pipe down? I—"

"Speaking of the blackout," Sarah said in a diplomatic tone. "The phone company sent someone around to check on us personally this morning. I thought that was so considerate, even if they are a couple of days late—"

Claire thought her head would split if she had to listen to any more inane family conversation. She pushed back her chair. "I'm going to take a nap."

"Don't you even want to finish your soup?" Burke asked.

She shook her head.

"I hope you wake up with a better personality," Nina said.

Claire didn't even respond. She left the dining room and walked heavily up the stairs.

Her bed looked cool and inviting. Claire pulled off her clothes and crawled between the sheets. But when she put her head on the pillow, she heard a crackling noise.

She sat up and slipped her hand into the pillowcase, thinking that it was probably a fabric softener sheet.

But it was a folded piece of paper. Claire stared at it in disbelief.

Do you ever dream of Wade, Claire?
In your dreams is he alive or dead?

"Okay, now we add the chives," Kate's mother said, brushing chopped chives off the cutting board with her long, manicured fingers. "Now we stir it a little more. . . ."

Kate watched her, amazed. Her mother seemed perfectly at home in the Cabrals' kitchen. In fact, seeing her be so natural with Mrs. Cabral for the past few days had been positively eye-opening. For example, right now her mother wasn't even wearing an apron to protect her beige silk blouse and linen skirt.

"Oh, wait," Mrs. Levin said. "I have to take off my rings for this part." She dumped her rings in the soap dish and began molding the cheese-and-chive mixture into a ball. "Now I roll it in chopped pecans and . . . voilà! Lunch."

Kate laughed. "We're having a cheese ball for lunch?"

Her mother smiled. "Well, you wanted me to cook for you, and this is the only thing I know how to make."

It struck Kate as appropriate that the only thing her mother knew how to make was a cheese ball. "I'll get some crackers," she said just as the kitchen timer went off.

"What's the timer for?" her mother asked.

Kate stiffened. "My medication."

Mrs. Levin looked absurdly pleased. "Really? I'm the one who first came up with that idea for you."

Yes, Kate thought gloomily, *and every time the timer goes off, I picture you, watching me like a hawk.*

She went to the sink for a glass of water and swallowed her pill. But when she turned around, her mother wasn't watching her, she was gazing out the kitchen door.

"It's so pretty here, Kate," she said softly. "I can see why you're so happy."

Kate picked a hangnail nervously. "Not *so* happy," she said quietly.

"But I thought—" Mrs. Levin said. "I thought since you had that Jake and everything—"

She still says "that Jake," Kate thought. *But she means "that alcoholic."*

"Oh, Kate," her mother said, her voice suddenly full of defeat. "I hate it when I see that sardonic look come over you and I know that you're thinking something unkind about me. I'm trying so hard, and I—I love you so much." Her mother didn't look at Kate when she said that. She began scraping the mixing bowl absently with the spatula. "I want more than anything to take you back to New York with me, but I know that's not what you want."

Kate remembered how just a few days before she'd wished for someone to lean on, someone with rock solid feelings for her. Her mother was still scraping the bowl with the spatula. Kate ran her finger around the edge of the bowl and tasted the cheese mixture thoughtfully.

"We could maybe try it for a while," she said.

Claire found Sarah and Janelle in the kitchen, going over the menus for the next week.

"What did he look like?" she asked Sarah.

"What did who look like?" Sarah said absently. "I think we'll have stuffed peppers on Thursday," she said to Janelle.

"The guy from the phone company," Claire said impatiently.

"Oh, heavens, I don't remember," Sarah said. "Why?"

"You must have some idea," Claire insisted. "He

was just here this morning. Young or old? Fat or thin?"

"Claire, why are you so interested?"

Janelle was studying Claire's face. "Is something missing from your room?"

Claire looked away. "No, I just wondered. . . . I thought maybe something had been moved around."

"Well, he may have moved furniture to check the lines," Sarah said. "I wouldn't worry. Now, what would you like for your farewell supper?"

"But what did he *look* like?" Claire asked.

"Claire, I wasn't interviewing him; I just answered the door," Sarah said.

"He was young," Janelle said, still looking at Claire intently. "He was . . . average looking. That's all I can remember."

Because he just blended in, right? Claire thought. *Because he was just perfectly nondescript. He specializes in that.*

She had one more question. "Did you see him leave?"

Janelle nodded. "Of course; I shut the door behind him myself."

Thank God, Claire thought.

"Now, dear," Sarah said again. "Do you have any requests for supper?"

"No, everything Janelle makes is delicious," Claire said automatically. Her attention was caught by something outside the kitchen window. The

Nortons had just pulled into their driveway and were unloading groceries from their island car.

Claire hurried out the kitchen door and across the street.

"Hi, Mr. Norton," she called as she reached their drive.

"Hi, Claire," he said, balancing a bag of groceries on his hip. "How are you?"

"Just fine, thanks," Claire said. "Hi, Mrs. Norton."

"Hello, Claire."

"I just wanted to ask you something. Did someone from the phone company come over to check your lines today?"

They both shook their heads. "Check our lines for what?" Mr. Norton asked.

"To make sure they were working after the blackout, I guess," Claire said.

"But it was the electricity that went out, not the phones," he said.

I didn't think of that, Claire thought. *I can't believe I didn't even* think *of that.*

"Why do you ask?" Mrs. Norton asked, tucking her hair more securely under her sun hat. "Did someone come to your house?"

Claire nodded. "I thought it seemed . . . suspicious."

"It certainly does," Mr. Norton said.

"You should call the phone company," Mrs.

Norton said. "If they didn't send a repairman, they should know that someone is passing himself off as one."

"Yes, I'll do that," Claire said, turning away. "Thank you."

She walked slowly back across the street, a shaky feeling in her stomach. *He was alone in the house with Janelle and Sarah,* she thought. *While I was off trying to keep an eye on my dad, he was here. How does he always know? And what if only one of them had been here? Or what if Nina had been here alone? Or—or me?*

She let herself into the house quietly and went upstairs and began searching. She found a note in the bathroom medicine cabinet that said, *What do you think Jake sees when he looks in the mirror?* Another was folded in among her lipsticks: *Lucas thought you were pretty enough to go to prison for, Claire. Too bad he couldn't see what you were really like.*

After that Claire stopped reading the notes. She collected as many as she could find and burned them.

Sixteen

"Hey, I thought the whole point of this bike ride was to be with Aisha," Lucas said, jerking his head toward the horizon, where Aisha appeared as no more than a speck. It had been Aisha's idea to come over to Weymouth and ride on this ten-mile trail. "And she left us behind in two seconds flat."

Zoey gave him a dark look. "Yes, the whole point *was* supposed to be about friendship," she said, looking meaningfully at Lara's back. Lara rode easily a few feet in front of them.

As though sensing the look, Lara suddenly dropped back until she was between Lucas and Zoey. "Why don't you like gazpacho, Zoey?" Lara asked conversationally.

Zoey looked irritated. "I don't know; I just don't."

"I love it," Lara said. "Your dad brought over a big bowl a few days ago, and we ate the whole thing between the two of us."

Lucas saw Zoey's eyebrows draw together, and

he quickly intervened. "I don't like gazpacho, either," he said lightly. "I don't like any cold soup. My mother used to make borscht, which is cold beets."

Neither girl responded, and they pedaled in silence for a minute.

"Hey, what color is your room?" Lara asked suddenly.

What the hell does she want to know that for? Lucas wondered. He didn't dare stop to give it much thought. Conversations between Zoey and Lara were too much like playing with sweaty dynamite: The slightest false move could trigger an explosion.

"Look, we should probably wait for Nina," Lucas said. "She's almost as far behind us as Aisha is ahead."

To his relief Lara rode a little bit ahead, but Zoey stopped her bike.

"Maybe we should walk for a while," she said. "I'd like to stretch my legs, anyway."

They walked their bikes slowly, one hand on the handlebars, their other hands clasped. Lucas squeezed Zoey's hand happily: She was still his, for the moment at least.

They rounded a corner of the bike path and stopped to admire the view. They could see a county fair just beginning to light up the Ferris wheel. "Oh, a fair," Zoey said softly. "I'd forgotten how many there are in August."

Lara rode back and circled them lazily. *Like*

a shark, Lucas thought sickly. He was glad when she rode a little way off again.

After about a minute Zoey said, "Here comes Nina."

Lucas watched as Nina wobbled into view. Because Lucas had lent Kate's bike to Lara, Nina had been forced to use her own bike, an old one-speed banana seat with ribbons on the handlebars. Lucas put the seat up as far as possible, but it was still basically a seven-year-old's bike. Aisha had laughed when she'd seen Nina on that bike, and the sound had been a relief to everyone.

Nina puffed up to them, her face bright red, and fell over into the grass, letting the bike drop onto her legs. "I can't go on," she said.

"Well, go ahead and rest a minute," Zoey said.

"A minute?" Nina said. "I could sleep from now until January—" She broke off suddenly. "Oh, a fair! I want some cotton candy."

"You do not want some cotton candy," Zoey retorted. "That stuff is like an instant cavity and five pounds all rolled into one."

"I don't care," Nina said. "I want some."

Lucas was surprised to hear himself speak. "We could go get some," he said. "That fair's not so far away."

Nina and Zoey looked at him in surprise.

"We could lock up the bikes," Nina said tentatively.

"What about Aisha?" Zoey said.
"She'll understand," Lucas said.
"What about Lara?"
All three looked at Lara's back.
"What about her?" Lucas asked.

Nina finished the last bite of her cotton candy. "So I'm stuck working in the office all *year,*" she said to Zoey.

Zoey considered, swallowing a bite of hot dog. She wiped her hands on her shorts. "Can't you just quit?"

"Are you kidding?" Nina asked. "After signing that contract? The Buzzard would probably take me to court. It would appear on my transcripts. It would probably keep me from getting into college!"

"Nina, calm down," Zoey said. "We'll think of something. At least you met Bradley."

"Yeah, I *met* him," Nina said. "But now he's flying off to Montana."

"Well, he must have liked you," Zoey countered. "Maybe he'll come back at Christmas."

"By Christmas I'll be a wizened little person," Nina said morosely. "My spirit crushed after months of tending to The Buzzard's every whim—"

She was interrupted by a cheer and the sound of a bell. Both girls turned to the booth where Lucas was pitching baseballs. He emerged from the crowd briefly and handed Zoey a small blue teddy bear. "I'll be right back; I want to get one for Nina, too," he said.

Nina smiled. If Zoey had prompted that, she would have resented it, but somehow it seemed natural and friendly for Lucas to say it.

Zoey was trying to stuff the teddy bear into her bum bag. "Isn't that Aisha's bum bag?" Nina asked suddenly.

"Yeah, why?"

"Well, when you return it to her, can you give her this tape?" Nina asked, pulling the cassette out of her pocket. "I keep forgetting."

"I guess so, sure," Zoey said. "What is it?"

"I don't know." Nina shrugged.

Zoey fitted it into the bum bag just as Lucas returned with another teddy bear, this one green, for Nina.

"Thanks," Nina said.

"Thanks, sweetie," Zoey said, kissing him.

"Come on, let's go on that baby roller coaster," Lucas said.

Both girls balked.

"I'm afraid of that roller coaster," Zoey said finally.

"I'm afraid of the man running that roller coaster," Nina said, eyeing him. "I don't think I'd trust him to put together a folding chair, let alone operate something life threatening."

Lucas ignored them and went up to a ticket booth. "Three, please," he said.

"Lucas!" Zoey protested. To Nina she said, "I've never understood what keeps you from falling out when it goes through the loop-the-loop."

"Centrifugal force," Lucas said, returning. He took them each by the elbow and steered them into line.

"Well, I know it's *called* centrifugal force," Zoey said. "But that doesn't mean I understand it. Or trust it," she added as a train of cars shuttled off down the track and the line crowded forward.

"I know what you mean," Nina said. "It's like when you ask someone how planes fly, and they tell you it's because planes are the same shape as paperweights."

"But paperweights don't fly," Zoey said.

"Well, exactly," Nina said.

"Oh, for God's sake, that's called the theory of aerodynamics," Lucas said. "When you two get together sometimes, the conversation completely deteriorates. Okay, here we go."

They were at the front of the line.

I'm going to throw up, Nina thought. *I just know it. Probably right when we're in the loop-the-loop. All that cotton candy. Some little kid will look up and say, "Mommy, what's that?" and point to a big pink sugary cloud—*

"Come on, Nina," Lucas said, guiding her into the car after Zoey.

Nina was uncomfortable. She didn't like sitting with her leg touching Lucas's, especially with Zoey on the other side of her.

But Zoey grabbed her hand and held it firmly, and Lucas grabbed the other one, and suddenly Nina didn't feel uncomfortable anymore; she just felt *included.* She held her breath as the car lurched forward.

"Oh, my God," Zoey said softly, and then they were off, climbing the track with dreadful slowness and flying down the hill into the loop-the-loop, where centrifugal force held them together as powerfully as friendship.

Aisha

I saw an interview with Roseanne once, and she said that money wasn't freedom to, money was freedom from. As in freedom from having a boring job and worrying about finances.

Well, that's how I feel about college. Like it's not going to be freedom to explore a whole new world of opportunities, it's going to be freedom from Christopher and wondering why he lied to me and how he could have betrayed me and the stupid reminders of him that are all over this dumb island I used to love.

I even feel that way about my future roommate. I mean, I hope she'll be nice and friendly, but mainly I hope she'll be quiet and studious and not completely wrapped up in guys

That's not how I wanted to feel about college And anyway, I'm not sure even college is going to make me stop thinking about him Today I ran my fastest ever mile and afterward (while I was rubbing BenGay into my legs) all I could think was, Wait until I tell Christopher!

And then of course, I realized that I wasn't going to tell Christopher, that the whole point of this stupid triathlon was to do something other than think of things to tell Christopher But it did occur to me I'll miss telling him a lot more than he'll miss hearing it If that makes any sense at all

Seventeen

Zoey barely noticed the jumble of duffel bags and cardboard boxes in the front hall. She assumed that it must be Benjamin's college junk as she stepped over it, but mainly she was too happy to give it much thought.

"Mom?" she called. "Dad? Sorry I'm late for supper."

Zoey was sorry that she was late, but it had been worth it. What a perfect afternoon, with both Nina and Lucas relaxed and happy for *once*. And it was just the three of them, without Lara, thank God. Zoey couldn't have planned a better afternoon.

"Hey, is anyone home?" she called again, coming into the dining room.

Her parents were sitting at the dining table, drinking cups of coffee. The plates from dinner were still on the table. Her mother didn't look happy.

"Mom, I'm so sorry," Zoey said. "I know I should have called, but we were having such a good time that I didn't think. Please don't be mad."

"I'm not mad at you, Zoey," her mother said. She emphasized the word *you* in such a way that made Zoey look closely at their faces for the first time. Her mother's was set and unhappy; her father's was determined.

"What?" she said, suddenly panicked. "What's going on?"

"Sit down," her father said.

"No." Zoey gripped the back of a chair. "Just tell me."

Her father hesitated. "Lara—"

"Lara!" Zoey interrupted. What now?

"Lara has been evicted from her apartment," Mr. Passmore said.

"So?" Zoey said, not caring if she sounded childish.

"Zoey," her father said patiently. "Lara is my daughter. I can't let her end up on the street."

Zoey looked at his face and guessed what was coming next. "So she's going to stay *here?*" Zoey said. "Great."

"I don't like it any better than you do," her mother said.

Mr. Passmore looked uneasy. "Zoey . . ." He paused, seeming to search for the right words. "Lara didn't want to stay in the garage apartment. She feels—and I agree with her—that it separates her too much."

"Who cares?" Zoey exploded. "Let her feel

separated. I *want* her to be separated. The garage apartment isn't separate *enough*. Where's she going to stay, then? In *my* room?"

She'd meant to be sarcastic, but she saw by her parents' faces that she was right.

"Oh, no," she said. "No way! I'd sooner you rented it out to some stranger while I was gone!"

Mr. Passmore looked pained. "Could you lower your voice, please?"

"Why?"

Then it clicked.

Zoey remembered the pile of luggage in the hall. She glanced at the table. Four plates. When she spoke, her voice was so terrible and calm, she barely recognized it. *"You mean she's already in my room?"*

"Zoey—"

"Thanks so much for clearing it with me," she said. "I hope you have a good night with her. I'll be finding someplace else to sleep."

"Honey—" Her mother spoke up.

"Good night, Mom," Zoey said, trying to make her voice less angry. She didn't say anything to her father.

She walked rapidly through the front hall, kicking Lara's junk out of her way. She hoped for some satisfying glass-breaking sounds, but everything seemed to be soft. Clothes, probably. It just made Zoey angrier.

She tried to slam the front door on her way out, but someone had latched it open to catch the evening breeze. Zoey struggled with the latch for a moment and then gave up, feeling as though she would scream if she stayed there another moment.

She walked away from her house without looking back. She was heading for sanctuary. She was heading for Lucas.

Claire sat across from Benjamin in Passmores' Restaurant, toying with a cup of split pea soup. *Soup is about all I can hold down these days,* she thought worriedly. *And only a tablespoon at that. What's going to happen to me?*

"The thing is," she said to Benjamin. "These notes were really personal, really private."

"They always have been," Benjamin pointed out.

"These were different," Claire said. "They were—*intimate.* He knew things about me."

"What kind of things?" Benjamin asked.

Claire hesitated. She wasn't ready to tell anyone, even Benjamin, about that awful note asking her if Wade was alive or dead in her dreams. He was neither, actually; in Claire's dreams he was always dying, and she could hear the blood bubbling in his lungs.

She shook her head. "Things about Wade and Lucas," she said evasively. "But *how* does he know these things?"

"He's obviously someone you know," Benjamin said.

"But then why doesn't anyone recognize him?" Claire asked. "People—Sarah, Janelle, others—have seen him, and they don't recognize him."

"Yes, but they don't know everyone you know," Benjamin said. "Maybe it's someone from school or something."

"But still . . . ," Claire said, struggling to find the right words. "He's—he's not afraid of being recognized."

The door to the restaurant opened, and Claire automatically looked up. That was her habit now. It was a middle-aged couple. As she glanced away she noticed a guy in the corner booth, smoking. She checked the brand of cigarettes. Marlboros.

She froze. *Oh, my God, that's him,* she thought. She took another look. He was wearing sneakers. He could have been the one who crept up behind her in the library that day.

Claire swallowed with a slight click in her throat.

"Benjamin," she said in a low voice, forcing a smile that she hoped would look natural from across the room. "Watch the guy wearing the baseball cap in the corner booth, okay? See if he looks at me."

She stood up and smoothed her skirt, all at once glad that she was wearing some of the new clothes she'd bought for college. She walked slowly across the room to the bar, swaying her hips slightly. She could feel her long dark hair swishing gently against the back of her pale pink blouse.

"Hello," she said to Mr. Passmore, who looked frankly startled.

He must be wondering what the slinky walk is all about, Claire thought.

She took a few napkins from the dispenser and turned around. She dropped one of the napkins and knelt slowly to retrieve it. The long flowered skirt she was wearing had a slit in it, and Claire knelt in such a way that her thigh was bare for at least thirty seconds.

"Oops," she said conversationally to Mr. Passmore as she stood up.

She walked slowly back to Benjamin and slid into the booth across from him.

"Well?" she asked.

"Not a flicker," Benjamin said. "Although my dad's eyes glazed over, and he looks like he needs to go lie down. What was that all about?"

Claire sighed heavily with disappointment. "I just thought that guy in the corner looked familiar," she said. "And I thought if I did something provocative—"

"I'll say," Benjamin said.

"—he would respond, but I guess not."

"I don't know," Benjamin said softly. "He was almost deliberately *not* watching you.

Everybody *else* was watching you. How does he look familiar?"

Claire frowned. "I don't know. It's almost like I knew him when he was much—"

She paused to think but couldn't come up with anything.

"Much different," she finished inadequately. "Oh, it's hopeless. I think I might be going insane—now I think *everyone* is the stalker."

She shoved the cup of soup away.

"Don't you want to finish that?" Benjamin asked.

"No," Claire said, wrinkling her nose. "It tastes like pesto."

"Mmmm," Benjamin nodded. "It's Dad's favorite new recipe."

Eighteen

Benjamin and Claire stood up to leave the restaurant together. Claire stopped at the register to pay for the soup.

"Are you coming back here, Benjamin?" Ms. Passmore asked.

He shook his head. "I'm kind of tired. I'm just going to walk Claire home and then go to bed."

"All right, sweetie," Ms. Passmore said. "But could you give us a call here if Zoey's home?"

I guess she didn't take the news about Lara sharing her room very well, Benjamin thought.

"Sure," he said.

"Lara went back to clean up her—other place," Ms. Passmore said awkwardly. Her lips tightened. "But she'll be back to spend the night."

On the sidewalk outside, Claire looked at him shrewdly. "Another headache?"

Benjamin thought about lying, but instead he nodded. "A bad one."

Claire looked torn, and he could tell she

wanted to ask him again to see a doctor, but she refrained. "You should go home and take some aspirin," she said.

"Let me walk you—"

"No," she said firmly. "I don't want you to strain yourself. I'll be fine, for heaven's sake. It's only a few blocks." Suddenly she kissed him on the cheek. "Go on home and take care of *yourself.*"

Benjamin smiled crookedly at her. The pain in his temples was astonishing. He watched her until the pale pink of her blouse faded into the dusk, and then he walked up the hill to his own house.

He opened the door. "Zoey?"

No answer.

"Lara?"

No answer.

Good. He just wanted to lie down. He grabbed a Coke from the fridge and headed upstairs, stopping at the bathroom for a bottle of aspirin.

He collapsed on his bed and took four aspirin with a mouthful of Coke. He had no idea if four aspirin were too many or not. He only knew that anything less sounded like too little.

He stretched to turn on the lamp by his bed. He didn't like being in total darkness, even when his head felt like it was splitting open.

He lay back, waiting for the aspirin to work, and that's when it happened: The window shade fell down across his left eye.

Benjamin tensed, his hands clutching involuntarily at the bedspread. *Okay,* he told himself. *Close your eyes and count backward from one hundred just like before. One hundred . . . ninety-nine . . . ninety-eight . . .*

Dimly he heard the front door open.

Oh, great, he thought. *That's Lara or Zoey. No matter which one it is, she'll want to talk, and I'm just not up to it.*

He listened as the footsteps circled the living room and dining room and headed for the kitchen.

Suddenly Benjamin's eyes snapped open. The window shade was still there, but he barely noticed. *Those footsteps are too heavy for Lara or Zoey,* he thought. *And they're unfamiliar.*

He slipped silently out of bed, his head pounding, and crept out in the hallway. It was completely dark. Night had fallen quickly.

Benjamin crept to the top of the stairs, keeping one hand against the wall for balance. The kitchen light was on, illuminating the foot of the staircase faintly. Benjamin had to close his left eye to see properly, altering his sense of depth perception, but even so he could make out the figure that walked past the staircase—and the dull gleam of the knife gripped in the figure's hand.

Almost before he was aware of what he was about to do, Benjamin whirled around and fumbled for the fuse box behind him. Frantically he threw the main switch, and his world plunged once again into darkness.

Aisha put the saucepan of milk on the stove to warm.

"What are you making?" Kalif asked.

"Warm milk to help me sleep tonight for the race tomorrow," Aisha said. "And hot cocoa for you if you do me a favor."

Kalif looked wary. "With as much chocolate syrup as I want?"

"Well, as long as there's more milk than syrup," Aisha said.

"Okay," he said happily. "What's the favor?"

Aisha held up her Walkman. "See this?" In her other hand she held up a cassette. "I want you to put this tape in this Walkman and hand them both to me in front of Weymouth City Hall tomorrow during the race."

He reached for them, but she held them out of reach. "This is important, Kalif."

"I promise, I promise."

"Okay." She handed him the Walkman and the tape. "Go watch TV. I'll bring the cocoa in when it's ready."

Kalif darted off happily, and Aisha shook her head. *Someday he'll figure out that he can microwave a cup of milk, and then he'll be harder to bribe,* she thought.

She was wearing a swimsuit, and she examined the abrasions on the inside of her thighs while she waited for the milk to heat up. *Running in a wet swimsuit is so disgusting,* she thought. *I wish I were fast enough to stop and change.*

The phone rang.

"Hello?"

"Could I speak to Aisha Gray, please?"

"This is she."

"This is Juliet Mitchell from the Harvard admissions office. I'm calling to apologize because we misplaced your file earlier and . . ."

Aisha frowned. Harvard calling *her?* At nine o'clock at night? To *apologize?* She didn't believe it for a second. She smelled Christopher behind this. Or that stupid Graham.

"Excuse me," she said. "What did you say your name was?"

"Juliet Mitchell."

"Are you calling me from the office?"

"Of course." Juliet sounded puzzled.

"Then I'll call you back in one minute," Aisha said, and hung up.

She took the milk off the burner and then dialed directory information.

"What city?"

"Cambridge, please."

"What listing?"

"I'd like the Harvard admissions office, please."

"Hold one minute for your number, ma'am."

Aisha wrote the number on the scratch pad by the phone. Then she hung up and dialed it. She got an automated recording. "Thank you for calling the Harvard admissions office. Please call again during our business hours. . . ."

Aha! Aisha thought.

". . . If you wish to leave a voice mail message, please dial the extension of the person you wish to speak to now, or dial one for the directory."

Aisha pressed one and then listened to the directory until she heard the name Juliet Mitchell. *I'll leave the real Juliet a message that someone's been impersonating her,* she thought, tapping in the extension.

"Admissions."

Aisha was startled. "Ju-Juliet Mitchell?"

"Yes?" It was the same voice.

"This is Aisha Gray again," Aisha said, gripping the kitchen counter for support. It really *was* Harvard.

"That was quick. Well, as I was saying," Juliet said. "Your file was set aside for consideration for the Julia B. Miles scholarship. Once the winner of that scholarship was decided, the files of the three people who qualified for it were not returned to the admissions office. In fact, you were to be the winner of that scholarship."

Oh, my God, Aisha thought.

"Unfortunately, after your file disappeared, it was mistakenly awarded to someone else," Juliet continued.

I don't believe this, Aisha thought weakly.

"But we *would* like to offer you the Melvin Richards scholarship, which is only for students of hard sciences from Maine."

"Melvin Richards scholarship?"

"Yes," Juliet said brightly. "Actually, we don't usually get to award this scholarship since our applicant pool from Maine is fairly limited. It covers residence and six thousand dollars tuition per semester."

Six thousand dollars, Aisha thought numbly. *Per semester. And residence.*

"Ms. Gray? Are you still there?"

"Yes, I'm here," Aisha said softly.

"Well, I understand that this is last minute and you need time to think about it," Juliet said. "But we'll need to hear back from you within twenty-four hours. Will that be possible?"

Aisha nodded, then realized that Juliet wouldn't be able to see that. "Yes," she said.

"Good. My number is—"

"I have your number."

"Oh, that's right. Well, good night, Ms. Gray."

"Good night." Aisha hung up. She was afraid to move away from the counter for fear she'd fall over.

After a minute or two she put the saucepan back on the burner, although she already knew she wasn't going to sleep at all that night.

Night fell quickly as Claire hurried home. She couldn't shake the feeling of apprehension. *Stop being so paranoid just because you thought you halfway recognized some guy in a restaurant,* she told herself. *You have plenty of other, more pleasant things to think about. You're leaving for college in two days, after all.*

She was leaving for college. It was an intimidating thought, and one she'd given almost no thought to because of the stalker. She assumed that the stalker knew she was going to MIT since he seemed to know everything else about her. She wondered if he would follow her. Probably. Even if he were someone local, Boston was only three hours away—

Claire froze.

She had thought that exact thought once before. She had been happy and full of anticipation. She had thought this: *Logan Airport's not so far away. Just three hours' drive. If things work out with this guy—*

Sean. She had thought that about Sean.

Sean, the guy she had met over the Internet and half fallen in love with. Claire had told him everything—about Wade, about Lucas, about

Jake. Every awful thing she'd ever done. And yet Sean had said that he could sense her regret, that he could see the good person she was underneath. Claire had agreed to meet him at Logan Airport. She'd had such high hopes, but then she saw Sean. And he was enormously fat.

"Oh, my God," she whispered.

Sean had been in the restaurant. She'd thought she'd known him when he was much different, and she had. She had known him when he was fat.

She had rejected him. She hadn't wanted to, she had been tempted to rise above something as trivial as outward appearances and focus on the Sean she knew from the Internet. But she just . . . couldn't. She was honest enough to realize that she would never be able to, and so she had—rejected him. There was no other way to put it.

Claire's skin was pale as paper and her eyes were huge as she stood alone on the street.

No wonder he always seemed to know what I was thinking. He did know! Because I told *him. All those times I thought he was just incredibly intuitive—he wasn't. He didn't have to be. I told him everything he could ever have possibly wanted to know.*

She turned around suddenly, sure that he would be in the dark street behind her. Maybe even *right* behind her—

But there was no one there.

Oh, God, she thought bleakly, squinting at the gloomy tree-lined street. *Of all nights for Benjamin not to walk me home.*

Benjamin! As clearly as though she were watching a film clip, Claire saw herself leaning up to kiss Benjamin's cheek.

Why did I do that? What did Sean think when he saw it? How did it make Sean feel?

She suddenly forgot all worries for herself and began running for the Passmores' house.

Nineteen

Benjamin kicked off his tennis shoes and waited at the top of the staircase. He guessed that Claire's stalker—for Benjamin had little doubt that it was anyone else—would head for the kitchen. Most fuse boxes were in the kitchen, and the stalker would figure Benjamin was there.

Benjamin would wait another minute and then slip down the stairs and out the front door and begin screaming bloody murder. The minute passed.

Benjamin began to descend the stairs. He had read in countless books that the silent way to go up or down stairs was to put your feet on the sides of the steps, near the wall. Benjamin knew that was nonsense. The *truly* silent way was to spend seven years as a blind person listening to other people climb up and down the stairs until every creak and groan was drilled into your memory and then avoid those spots.

Benjamin came down the stairs so quietly, the air barely moved. He knew exactly how many stairs there were, and so he wasn't surprised when his stocking foot hit the marble of the hallway. It was just five steps to the front door.

Benjamin put out his hand to feel the wall.

Instead he felt the warm skin of the stalker's face.

Lucas was already showered and in his pajama bottoms when he heard a knock on the screen door.

"Come in!" he called from the kitchen.

Zoey opened the door and stepped inside.

"Zoey!" he called. "Come into the kitchen. I'm making a sandwich. Aren't you starved? Are your folks mad—"

He broke off as she came closer and he saw her expression. Her eyes were wet, and her nose had that sort of red, rabbity look that was always a precursor to crying.

"Where have you been?" she asked. "I came around and knocked half an hour ago, and you weren't here."

"I was taking a shower," he said absently. "What's wrong?" He put down the mustard jar.

"Oh, Lucas, it's awful," Zoey whispered. A tear slid down her cheek.

"Oh, babe," Lucas said. He put his arms around her, and she buried her face against his bare chest. "What is it?"

Zoey sniffed. "Lara."

A cold finger of dread slid down Lucas's spine. Had Lara told? Was Zoey coming over here to lay the whole story out in front of him and ask him to deny it? Was he going to have to look her in the eye and *lie?*

"What about Lara?" he asked thickly.

"She's moving into my room!" Zoey sobbed. "And my dumb, stupid father told her she could!"

Relief made Lucas light-headed. He clutched Zoey tighter.

"All because she's getting evicted from her apartment," Zoey continued. "Well, that's *her* fault. Let her find another apartment."

"Is she there now?" Lucas asked.

"Yes!" Zoey said. "My dad didn't even ask before he just moved her on in."

Damn Mr. Passmore, Lucas thought. What was he going to do? He couldn't risk totally siding with Zoey and then having Lara somehow find out.

"Zo, sweetie," he said carefully, stroking her hair. "Your dad was way, way out of line not to ask you first, but . . . you're leaving the day after tomorrow."

"So?" Zoey said, still muffled against his chest. "It's still *my* room. It's still the room I want to come home and spend holidays in, and now Lara will probably be there forever."

"I know your room is important to you

because it's the room you grew up in," Lucas said. "But it's really just a room, and—"

Zoey pulled away from him, her blue eyes blazing. "So what are you saying? That I'm being childish?"

"No, I—"

"Isn't it interesting how everyone thinks I'm being an unreasonable baby, and yet *I'm* the one who has to share my room with someone I can't stand."

Lucas couldn't fault her there. "But Lara's—improving," he said, hating himself. "You can't see it, but—"

Zoey narrowed her eyes and wiped her nose on the back of her hand. "Thanks for all the sympathy and understanding," she said deliberately.

"Zoey—"

"What exactly is with you and Lara these days?" she said, still staring at him. "You and Lara and *Nina,* I should say, because she's doing it, too."

"Doing what?" Lucas asked, panic rising inside him.

"Defending Lara," Zoey said slowly, obviously thinking. "Or sort of half defending her. No, not that. It's almost like you're—you're both—"

Scared of her, Lucas thought. *Scared. That's the word you're looking for.*

The phone rang.

He had never been happier for an interruption in his life. Because if Zoey figured out that he and Nina were scared of Lara, she wouldn't rest until she knew why.

"Hello?" he said. "Yes, Ms. Passmore, she's right here."

He handed Zoey the phone. His hand was so sweaty, he left big sticky fingerprints on the receiver.

He didn't move, Benjamin realized suddenly. *When the lights went out, he stopped and waited for me to come to him. Thank God he was facing the other way—*

He didn't have time to think further. He saw the flash of the knife and reflexively put up his hand and closed his fingers around the blade.

The knife went through his palm and Benjamin could feel it—could actually *feel* it—scraping at the bones. He screamed and shook his hand viciously. The knife withdrew from his flesh with a horrible wet sucking noise.

Benjamin fell sideways onto the marble floor, and the pain in his hand sharpened his instincts. He rolled in the direction of the stairs and was running up their carpeted softness within seconds. But he could hear footsteps right behind him.

He ran up both flights to Zoey's room, going faster than he would have thought possible, his hand sending a bolt of pain along his arm with every step. He burst into Zoey's room, intent on hiding in the wooden alcove, when his hip hit her desk and the screen saver on her laptop came to life, bathing the room in bright blue light.

Jesus Christ! Benjamin thought frantically. His uninjured hand flew out and slammed the laptop shut. The door opened behind him, and Benjamin hurled himself away into darkness.

He landed silently, cushioned by all sorts of soft things on the floor. Lara's clothes, he thought dimly. He curled himself into as small a ball as possible in the alcove.

The stalker doesn't know this room, he thought, trying not to pant. *If you don't know the room, you would never know this was here. All I have to do is wait. He can't afford to stay here forever.*

He listened, but he couldn't hear any footsteps. The stalker was standing still again, probably waiting for his eyes to adjust to the darkness.

Benjamin couldn't see any lights blinking on Zoey's laptop. *I must have turned it off or broken it when I slammed it,* he thought. *I forgot that damn thing ran on batteries. But I haven't forgotten anything else—*

And then he heard the low humming noise as the generator kicked on.

* * *

The Passmores' front door was slightly ajar. Claire pushed it open and stepped inside. It was dark. She flicked the light switch, and nothing happened.

Sean's already been here, she thought with a sinking heart. *He's cut the electricity.*

She pushed the door farther open so that light from the street lamps spilled in. She saw the dark stains by the staircase. They looked black in the dim light, but Claire had no doubt that they were really red.

I'm too late, she thought frantically. *I should run for the police, an ambulance—*

But suddenly she felt not fear but anger, and overwhelming anger.

She left the door and headed up the stairs, gripping her purse with hands that didn't tremble. *We'll see who's afraid when I find you,* she thought. *You can run, but you can't hide.*

Claire reached the first landing. Should she go into Benjamin's room? She knelt and felt the first step on the stairs that led to Zoey's room. A faint wet spot.

She straightened up and climbed those stairs as well.

What is that humming? she thought with annoyance. *How will I hear Sean or find Benjamin with that humming in my ears?*

The lights flickered on. Claire almost

screamed with surprise, but she didn't have time.

Sean was right there! He was in front of her, in the doorway to Zoey's room. She'd been within inches of bumping into him. Over his shoulder Claire could see Benjamin crouched on the floor with blood all over his shirt.

Suddenly, things seemed to be happening in slow motion. Sean raised the knife and took a step forward. Claire tried to scream Benjamin's name, but no sound came out. She reached into her purse, and drew out the hammer. It seemed to take an eternity, but she raised it high over her head, and brought it down on Sean's head with more force than she would have thought possible.

His skull made a distinctly inhuman wooden splintering sound. It was a sound Claire would remember for the rest of her life.

Sean took one step forward. He tried to take another and tripped over a rolled-up sleeping bag. His neck bent, and he landed so that he was staring at Claire. She felt her face contort into what must have been a horrible expression. The rage completely overwhelmed her.

Claire stepped over the sleeping bag and raised her hammer again. A hand closed over her wrist. It was Benjamin.

"That's enough, Claire," he said softly.

She struggled to free the hammer. "Let go!"

"I said, that's enough," he said more forcefully. "What do you want to do—kill him?"

Claire stared at him, panting.

Neither one of them said anything else.

"Look, Mom," Zoey was saying into the phone, "I don't want to stay away, either, but I just refuse to share my room with that viper. . . . No, I don't think the use of the word *viper* is being melodramatic. . . . Well, if Dad loves her all that much, why doesn't she sleep in *your* room. . . . I don't know, maybe in a basket at the foot of your bed. . . . Stop laughing, that wasn't a joke. . . . I don't—hey, do you hear a siren?"

Lucas put his hand on her shoulder. "It sounds like it's heading to your house," he said.

Twenty

Zoey dunked her scrub brush in the bucket of soapy water and watched the water turn pink. She slapped the brush back down on the blood-stained carpet. She had to squeeze her eyes shut against the memory of arriving at the house at the same time as her frantic parents . . . Benjamin leaving the house with the paramedics, his shirt drenched with blood and his face pale . . . Claire talking to the police and absently clutching a hammer with blood and hair stuck to it . . . Zoey searching for a T-shirt for Claire to wear because the police wanted to test the blood pattern on Claire's pale pink blouse . . . the light on top of the police car shining red against the wall, then disappearing, shining, then disappearing . . .

"So whose blood have you got over there?" Lara asked, interrupting her thoughts.

Zoey cleared her throat. "Benjamin's, I think."

"Well, whose am I cleaning up, then?"

Zoey scrubbed at the stain. "Sean's."

"Who's Sean again?" Lara plunged her own scrub brush into her own bucket.

"I'm still not one hundred percent clear on that," Zoey confessed. "Apparently some guy who's been terrorizing Claire."

"Oh," Lara said. "I didn't know she was being terrorized."

"Neither did I," Zoey said. "She didn't tell anyone."

"Where's Sean now?"

"In the trauma unit at the hospital, I guess."

"Oh," Lara said. "I wish your parents would call. It's been hours."

"I wish they would, too, but it's a long trip to the hospital," Zoey said, thinking of her parents and Benjamin at the emergency room.

Lara threw her brush in the bucket and rubbed the small of her back. "Look, I just don't think this is going to come out. It's worse than the spaghetti-vomit stain in my old apartment."

Zoey pushed her hair off her face. "Well, maybe a throw rug or something."

"It'll take about five throw rugs," Lara said. "And then it will look like stepping-stones." She looked at Zoey suddenly. "You know, you're taking me moving into your room better than I thought you would."

Better than you hoped *I would, you mean,* Zoey thought wryly.

She shrugged. "I was upset at first. But then, with all that's happened, I just realized how lucky I am—"

She broke off at the sound of the front door opening.

She and Lara both jumped to their feet and raced downstairs. Benjamin was in the hallway, looking pale and tired but relieved, his bandaged hand held carefully in front of him.

Zoey's parents also looked pale but relieved. "No nerve damage," Zoey's mother said happily. "Just a few stitches."

"Oh, Benjamin," both girls cried, and rushed to throw their arms around him.

"His hand!" shouted Mr. Passmore.

"My hand!" shouted Benjamin, holding it above his head.

Zoey and Lara hugged him, anyway, and looking at the relief on Lara's face, Zoey thought, *Perhaps we do have something in common after all.*

Claire finished the last slice of pizza. "Don't you have anything else?" she asked the detectives. "Some doughnuts, a sandwich, a packet of sugar? I'll eat anything." She laughed. "I haven't had an appetite in *weeks.*"

The detective closed his notebook. "Actually you're free to go now, Miss Geiger," he said. "I think you've answered all our questions. Your father's waiting for you downstairs."

"Oh," Claire said. "Okay." She pushed back her chair.

"Miss Geiger," the detective said.

"Hmmm?" she said, smiling at him. She was so happy, so lighthearted, so relieved.

"This kind of thing can be very traumatic, very stressful," the detective said. "People can have . . . flashbacks and that kind of thing. If you'd like to see a therapist, we can recommend a good one."

Claire stood up and brushed the pizza crumbs off her skirt. "I'll be fine, thanks anyway." She began walking toward the exit.

"Don't you even want to know how he's doing?" the detective asked. "Sean? Don't you want to know if he makes it?"

"No," Claire said. Then she thought the better of it. "Tell me if he dies."

Lara lay on the trundle next to Zoey's bed and stared at the stupid artificial stars on the ceiling. It was three in the morning, and they were just going to bed.

Zoey sighed restlessly in the other bed. The trundle bed was about a foot lower than Zoey's bed, so Lara couldn't see her, but she could hear that she was awake.

"Can't you sleep?" Lara asked.

"No," Zoey said, sighing again. "Too much on my mind, I guess."

Like what? Lara thought. *How you're going to arrange the stars on your dorm-room ceiling?*

"Like what?" she said aloud.

"Oh . . ." Zoey sounded caught off guard. "Lucas, mainly, I guess. I wasn't very nice to him about—something tonight."

Me, Lara thought. *They fought about me.* She smiled in the dark.

"And I should be nice to him," Zoey continued. "Because he's always been so completely supportive of me. I mean, I'm going five million miles away to college the day after tomorrow, and I don't have the slightest worry about him."

Lara's lips tightened. *God, you are sickening,* she thought.

She thought about Lucas and Nina and Zoey ditching her on the bike ride. Why should she protect Lucas after a stunt like *that?* And then Zoey saying, *I realized how lucky I am.* As if everyone didn't already *know* how very lucky Zoey was.

And now she had to listen to Zoey drone on about how wonderful Lucas was and how bad she felt for being a little teeny bit mean to him.

Lara sat up suddenly. "Zoey?"

"Hmmm?" Zoey was lying on her side in her

dumb Boston Bruins jersey. Her blond hair was fanned out softly on the pillow.

"I don't know how to tell you this," Lara said. "But Lucas isn't what you think he is."

Zoey lifted her head slightly. "What do you mean?"

"I mean, he's not—trustworthy," Lara said. "He's been making out with Nina behind your back ever since you left for Washington."

Zoey didn't bat an eyelash. "You're lying."

"No, I'm not," Lara said. She switched on the bedside lamp so that she would be able to see it in Zoey's eyes when she finally believed.

Twenty-one

Zoey pulled on a pair of jeans and an old gray T-shirt.

"Zoey—" Lara began.

"Leave me alone," Zoey said. "Shut up."

"I just thought you should know," Lara said.

Zoey stared at her coldly. "I am not a fool," she said. "I know you enjoyed telling me. I could see it in your face. Now, take your pillow and your blanket and go down to the couch. Just—stay—away—from—me."

Lara shrugged. She gathered up her bedding while Zoey tucked in her T-shirt. Lara paused in the doorway. "You do believe me, though, don't you?" she asked.

"Yes," Zoey said grimly. "I believe you."

Lara left, and Zoey sank down on the edge of her bed.

Yes, she believed Lara. She didn't want to, but it was amazing how the truth solved so many little mysteries from the past weeks.

She remembered the night she'd found

Lucas and Nina embracing in the backyard. Lucas had said he was comforting her, that Nina was upset over Benjamin.

It seemed reasonable at the time, Zoey thought, but now she felt like a fool for believing it.

She wanted to feel angry, but she could only feel hurt. Lucas and Nina! Nina and Lucas! Zoey buried her face in her hands. *What am I going to do?* she thought. *How could they? How could they do that to me? I thought they loved me.*

She *was* a fool. She was the biggest fool who ever lived. Anyone else would have realized something was going on. Zoey cringed when she thought of how distant Lucas had been when she returned, how strangely Nina had behaved. *I thought it was just because I'd been away,* she thought bitterly. *But it was really because I'd come back.*

She thought about kissing Lucas and swallowed shakily. She'd been ready to go further than ever before with him, and he'd seemed unsure. Lucas unsure about going too far! That was a joke. He was only unsure about how he felt about Zoey, clearly.

And then they tried to cover it up! *Were they going to tell me when I was off in California?* she wondered. *Were they such cowards that they were going to wait until I was safely on another coast?*

They could have at least told me themselves,

Zoey thought. *They could have had the* courage *to tell me themselves.* Instead they had let her hear it from Lara. They had let her truly be the last to know.

Have they been laughing at me? Zoey wondered suddenly. *All three of them?*

She stood up and went into the bathroom to splash cold water on her face. Her skin was blotchy, and her eyes were red from crying. She didn't care.

Back in her bedroom she chose her two heaviest duffel bags and put the straps over her shoulders. It was lucky that she was almost finished packing. Awkwardly she carried them down the still dark stairs to her parents' room.

Zoey knocked. "Mom? Dad?" There was no answer. She pushed open the door. "Mom?"

Her mother rolled over sleepily and squinted. "Zoey? Is something wrong?"

Zoey switched on the light. Mr. Passmore groaned and pulled the pillow over his head.

"Mom, Dad," Zoey said. "I need you to do me a favor and not ask any questions."

Her father pushed the pillow off his face, and her mother sat up. "Zoey—"

"You're going to think I'm crazy," Zoey said. "And this will probably be expensive, but I need you to drive me to Boston right now and put me on the first plane to California."

*   *   *

Christopher woke up, as he did most mornings, to the annoying sound of Kendra singing in the shower.

He reached over and pounded on the thin wall. "Stop it!" he shouted. "Some people are meant to sing professionally, some people only in the shower, and some people not at all. You're in the last category."

"Jeez, okay," Kendra muttered over the splashing of the water.

"Don't you speak to me!" Christopher shouted. "You know the rules. I talk to you, but you never talk to me. Never. And I want you to turn and look at the wall when I pass you in the hall."

"That is the most idiotic—"

"Kendra!" He thumped the wall again.

"I was talking to myself," Kendra protested.

"Well, you're not now," Christopher said. "So shut up."

He slumped back down in bed grumpily. The numbers on his old digital clock shuffled audibly. 6:05. Christopher groaned.

This was the last day before Aisha left for Princeton. The last day for her to tell him that she had listened to the tape and that she forgave him.

Christopher sighed. He knew that wasn't going to happen. She would have gotten in touch with him long before this. Obviously she had listened to the tape and she couldn't forgive him for what he'd done.

And yet—and yet she was acting peculiar. Christopher had expected to hear from her either way. Aisha had such a temper. It wasn't like her not to speak her mind. When he'd seen her at the Pressmans' pool, he'd expected her to let loose: *You are the weakest, least-principled person I have ever known. . . .*

But there'd been none of that. Only a kind of hurt, prideful silent treatment. Christopher shook his head. He would never understand women. Not in a million years. Like Aisha running in that triathlon. What was that all about?

He lost himself briefly in a fantasy of Aisha in a swimsuit. And then it occurred to him that he could go see Aisha, the real Aisha, in her swimsuit. He was allowed to watch the race, after all. It was a free country.

Aisha stood shivering on the cement boat dock along with twenty other idiots in swimsuits. It was seven in the morning, but a crowd had already gathered.

The eleven pinned to the back of her suit itched, and Aisha shrugged irritably. She shook her legs, trying to loosen the muscles. Mainly she just shivered.

God, she thought, *the* air *is cold. What's the* water *going to be like?*

She rubbed her arms and studied the two

buoys posted in the bay. It was a "triangular open-water sea swim," according to the booklet. The booklet also said that "individuals wearing wet suits will be regarded as using a flotation device and disqualified."

Yes, Aisha thought sarcastically. *And individuals not wearing wet suits will be allowed to lose feeling in their limbs and sink to the bottom of the bay.*

The cutoff time for the swim race was ninety minutes, which seemed a little pointless to Aisha because after ninety minutes in that water, a person's body temperature would be—

"One minute to start, swimmers!" an official yelled.

Swimmers? Aisha thought hysterically. *Is there a swimmer in the crowd? Nope.*

Good God, why was she *doing* this? If she accepted that Harvard scholarship, she would get more than ten *times* the first prize for this dumb triathlon, and that was just one semester.

Aisha imagined how happy her dad would be if she could say casually, "Oh, don't worry about tuition, Dad. I've got a scholarship."

But she couldn't say that, because she wasn't going to Harvard, she was going to Princeton. She was going to put as many miles as possible between herself and Christopher. She wished she had applied to the University of Alaska.

"On your mark!" shouted the official.

Aisha lined her toes up on the edge of the boat dock and bent her knees.

"Go!" shouted the official.

Aisha pushed off with her legs. Her hands broke the surface of the water in a firm V.

In the split second before her head hit the water, Aisha caught a dizzying upside-down view of the crowd. The crowd—and one face in particular.

Christopher? she thought, and then the icy water closed over her.

Twenty-two

Kalif was racing for the ferry. Aisha would scalp him if he missed it and wasn't there in time to meet her in front of city hall.

He was running so fast, he ran right into Benjamin.

"Hey, Kalif," Benjamin said. "Just the man I'm looking for."

"You're looking for me?" Kalif asked, surprised. He didn't think he'd ever had a conversation with Benjamin.

"Could you give this to Aisha?" Benjamin asked, holding out a cassette. "My sister Zoey asked me to give it to her."

Kalif closed his hand over the tape. "Is it her running tape?"

"I don't know," Benjamin said. "Maybe."

"Aren't you going to the race?" Kalif asked.

Benjamin shook his head. "No, I don't feel too good."

Kalif didn't doubt it, not with that bandage on his hand and that fire spot in his eye.

* * *

Aisha splashed out of the water, still shivering, and tried to make her legs run toward the parking lot that held their bikes. Her legs resisted; they felt like lengths of rope.

She jogged along stiffly, water streaming off her. She checked her watch: The swim had taken her thirty-seven minutes.

Amazing what a big motivator a little subzero water can be, Aisha thought. She still wasn't in the lead, though.

She found her bike under a sign marked 11 and climbed onto it, grimacing as water squeezed out of her swimsuit and drenched the bike seat. She slammed on the regulation helmet and began pedaling out of the parking lot.

The booklet also had a lot of amusing terminology for the bike race. For example, it called the hills "challenging." Aisha had her own word for the hills, and it wasn't nearly as positive. And the booklet referred to the half mile of gravel road that started the bike race as a "special feature." Aisha referred to it as "sadistic."

She left the parking lot, turned right, hit the gravel road, and nearly fell over. There was that face in the crowd again: Christopher.

Nina met Lucas going up the Passmores' driveway. "Hey," he said, smiling. He nodded at the roll of computer printout paper under her arm. "Is that a banner for Aisha?"

Nina smiled self-consciously. "Yeah. I thought we could hold it up in front of city hall."

"What does it say?"

She unrolled it for him, holding it awkwardly with her arms spread out.

"Eesh, Eesh, Eesh," he read. "That sounds like an old man complaining."

"I know," Nina said, exasperated. "But *you* try working 'Aisha' into a cheer of some sort."

"Oh," Lucas said. "I see your point."

Nina began folding up the banner.

"Nina?"

"Hmmm?" she said absently.

"We have to tell Zoey the truth."

Nina dropped the banner. "The truth?" she said. "The truth about us?"

He nodded.

"Oh, Lucas, no," Nina said desperately. "We can't. She'll never forgive us. She'll never look at us the same way. I don't want her to hate us—"

"She'll hate us more if she hears it from Lara," Lucas said. He put his hands on Nina's shoulders. "I was up all night, thinking. We have to tell her."

Nina looked at the ground miserably. "Today?"

"I think so," Lucas said, looking her squarely in the face. "I don't want to have to tell Zoey something like this over the phone while she's in California."

"I know," Nina said. "I know you're right.

We should have told her a long time ago."

He let go of her shoulders, and they went up and knocked on the Passmores' front door. There was no answer.

"Should we knock again?" Lucas asked. "I hate to wake them up after everything they went through last night."

"I know," Nina said, "but Zoey wouldn't like it if we went without her, since it's her last day."

Lucas knocked again, and this time Lara answered, looking sleepy. She had a blue blanket wrapped around her shoulders. "What?" she demanded ungraciously.

"Is Zoey up?" Lucas asked.

Lara yawned daintily, covering her mouth. "You just missed her."

"You mean she left for Weymouth already?" Lucas said.

"I mean she left for California," Lara said.

"California?" Nina said. "She's not leaving until tomorrow."

Lara shrugged. "Well, she decided to go early."

Nina frowned. Fear brushed close by her, like a fish underwater. "Why?"

"I don't know," Lara said. An impish look crossed her face. "Maybe—maybe she heard some upsetting news."

Oh, my God, thought Nina. *Lara told her.* She thought she was going to faint.

Lucas lunged for Lara, but Lara was quicker and slammed the door. Lucas pounded on it with his fist. "Open up! *Open up*—"

"Lucas!" Nina said softly, urgently. She grabbed his hand. "The ferry! Let's go!"

That brat, Aisha thought viciously, scanning the crowd for Kalif. *That stupid little snot-nosed brat.*

She would kill Kalif. It was as simple as that. No court in the land would convict her after she explained about the chafing from the wet swimsuit. She would say, *My little brother was supposed to hand me a Walkman to help keep my mind off the chafing, and he forgot*—

The hand with the Walkman in it popped out in front of her so abruptly she almost ran into it. She grabbed the Walkman reflexively and caught a glimpse of Kalif's sweaty, worried face. She gave him a quick smile, and then she was past him.

That wonderful, wonderful kid, she thought, fumbling the headphones onto her ears.

She pressed play, but instead of the Spice Girls she heard a lot of scratching and clicking. *Oh, God, he gave me the wrong tape,* she thought. *If this is New Kids on the Block, I'm going to scream.*

More clicking and then a voice saying, *"Eesh, uh, I called you today, and your dad said you had a message for me, which was that you had joined the foreign legion. . . ."*

Aisha stumbled and stared at the Walkman as though it had betrayed her.

Christopher?

Lucas and Nina pounded down the landing, even though the ferry was at least a hundred yards out to sea.

"Zoey!" Lucas shouted.

He and Nina ran right up to the edge of the landing.

They could see the Passmores on the ferry, all three of them, looking back toward North Harbor.

"Zoey!" Lucas shouted as loud as he could. "Zoey!"

"Zo!" Nina screamed next to him.

Zoey couldn't have failed to hear them, much less see them, but she gave no sign. She simply stood there, looking at them, her fair hair blowing in the wind. The look of sadness on her face was indescribable.

"Zoey!" Lucas shouted again, although he knew it was pointless.

It was over. She was gone.

Aisha's feet slapped against the hot pavement. Her skin chafed against the swimsuit. She didn't care. She was too busy listening.

. . . I watched as Carina's dark eyes became at ease and happy, and when I looked up, the girl had turned her face to me. "You ready?" she said.

I looked at this girl, this girl who looked so untrustworthy that I wouldn't want her to be my waitress, and I thought, Are you crazy?*—and then I saw Carina.*

She was leaning forward, watching me, and her eyes were shining. She was looking at the bag. Then she raised her eyes and smiled at me, a bright hot smile.

I told the girl I was ready. . . .

I would have done anything for her in that moment, Aisha. Anything.

I sat there thinking about where I was, about who I had married, about what I was doing. . . .

Aisha was nearing the finish line. A blister on her heel broke. A muscle twinged in her left calf, threatening to cramp.

Aisha noticed none of these things. She was at that party with Christopher three years ago.

. . . I—I fainted. Out cold. I flopped backward, and I guess I must've bashed my head on the headboard or something because there was a big goose egg on my temple later.

I came to about a minute later, and all I

could think of was, Oh, my God, did they inject me? "Did you inject me?" I said to the girl. "Did you?"

She gave me a disgusted look. "No, I don't inject unconscious people. It's a waste."

Carina wouldn't even look at me, but I could tell by her posture that she was furious. I didn't care. I ripped the rubber tubing off my arm and went home, leaving her there. She didn't come home—at least she wasn't home by five in the morning, which was when I finished packing my bags and left.

I felt sick. I couldn't believe what I'd almost let Carina do to me. No, that's not accurate. I couldn't believe what I *had been* willing *to do for Carina. I hated drugs. I've seen what they can do, I've watched them kill people in my neighborhood, I've seen drugs destroy people, marriages, entire families . . . and yet I had been willing to do* heroin *for Carina. For a long time I thought I might as well have done it since it wasn't any act of willpower that prevented me. I just fainted.*

Anyway, I moved back to my mom's, and the marriage was annulled and I never saw Carina again. I can't possibly be the father of Carina's baby because after that night I never felt anything like desire for her again, and that was three years ago. But I heard about her. I heard—things. That she was getting deeper and deeper into drugs. And once I thought I saw her, standing on a corner in a hooded sweatshirt. But maybe it was just a girl waiting for a bus and not Carina waiting for . . . well, not the bus.

I swore I would never let anyone—any girl—have so much power over me again. I steered pretty clear of any relationship that required commitment . . . and then I met you.

I thought I could keep you at arm's length, but I was wrong. And then I thought I could just blot out the past, pretend it had never happened. I wish it never had. But it did, and you deserve to know about it. I should have told you a long time ago, but I couldn't bear to have you know how weak I am.

If I don't hear from you, I'll know that you don't want to have anything to do with me, and I'll understand.

But I do love you, Aisha. I really do.

Aisha passed the finish line. The official clicked his stopwatch and announced her time, but she wasn't listening. She didn't even stop running.

Her legs, which by now felt like twin pillars of wet sand, carried her twenty feet beyond the finish line. She cleared the barricade easily and crowded in among the spectators, where she threw her arms around Christopher and pressed her sweaty, sandy self against him as though she could never get close enough.

Twenty-three

They said good-bye, all of them, in the ferry parking lot, on a cool gray windy morning, made colder and grayer by Zoey's absence.

The only truly happy people were Aisha and Christopher, who arrived holding hands and would have been surrounded by singing birds and floating hearts if such things existed outside of *Cinderella.*

Nina took one look at them and said, "On?"

Aisha nodded happily. "Very much so."

"What's on?" Burke asked.

Aisha put her arms around Christopher's waist. "Our engagement."

"Well, congratulations," Burke said. "Although I never knew it was off. Congratulations also on the triathlon. I hear you came in fourth."

"Yes," Aisha said. "I got a ham."

"A what?" Burke asked.

"A ham. I got a ham for a prize," Aisha said. "They tried to make it sound more exciting by going on and on about it being sugar cured and all, but there really wasn't much they could do to disguise the fact that it *was* a ham."

"What'd you do with it?" Claire asked.

"I traded it with my parents," Aisha said. "They're serving it for brunch in exchange for letting Christopher use their car to drive me to Harvard."

"Harvard?" asked Mr. Passmore, overhearing. "I thought you were going to Princeton."

"It's a long story," Aisha said. "I just decided I'd rather be closer to home." She looked at Christopher and smiled.

"Well," Nina said. "I'm sorry all you got was a ham after you trained so hard."

"Oh, I'd do it again in a minute," Aisha said. "In a heartbeat." She looked at Christopher, and they smiled about something Nina didn't understand.

"Well, kids," Mr. Gray said. "I suppose you should be setting off." He gave the keys to Aisha.

"Hey, don't you think I should drive?" Christopher said.

"He's afraid I'm going to get a cramp and accelerate straight into a wall," Aisha said, laughing.

"It's possible," Christopher said.

Mr. Gray didn't look nearly so amused about the potential destruction of his automobile. "Now, look, you have to be careful," he said. "My insurance will go sky-high if—"

"Dad, please stop saying that every two seconds," Aisha said, hugging him. "Though it's kind of nice to have you back to normal. Now go on home and relax. Have some ham."

"Hey, where's Zoey?" Jake asked the Passmores.

"She left yesterday," Mr. Passmore said.

"Yesterday!" Jake's face darkened. "Without saying good-bye to me? Why?"

"She just decided she had to," Mr. Passmore said.

Lucas and Nina stared at the ground.

"Well, there must have been a reason."

Mr. Passmore cleared his throat. Everyone else looked away.

"Jake?" Claire called from over by the Geigers' BMW. "Could you come give me a hand?"

Nina tried not to give a big noisy sigh of relief.

Jake walked over to Claire. "Can you fit this into the trunk?" she asked, indicating a box at her feet.

Jake lifted the box, grunted, and began struggling to wedge it into the already packed trunk. "What's in here, anyway?" he asked as he pressed it into place. "Gold bars?"

"Very funny," Claire said.

Jake straightened. "There you go."

"Thanks," she said. She held out her hand. "Good-bye, Jake. Good luck at school."

He held on to her hand. "You too . . . and Claire?"

"Yes?"

"I heard about Sean and what happened last night. I'm sorry that had to happen to you."

She lifted her shoulders and gave him a tiny smile. "It's over now."

"Still, it must've been a hell of a thing to go through," Jake said. "And having it end the way it did. With the . . ."

"Hammer," Claire finished flatly.

Jake nodded. "You must not have slept a wink last night."

Claire looked at him with genuine puzzlement. "I slept just fine," she said.

Benjamin walked over to where Claire stood, leaning against the Geigers' BMW. She wore linen shorts and a crocheted T-shirt and looked incredibly beautiful. He had his camera around his neck and considered taking her picture but didn't.

"Hi," he said softly.

"Hi," she said. "Or bye, really." She looked at his left eye. "What's that bloody spot?"

"I don't know," he said. He resisted the urge to touch his eye. "But I have an appointment with a specialist in Manhattan on Wednesday."

Her face lit up. "You do? Really?"

"Really," he said. "It just seemed easier to do it where no one knows me. No one even knows I'm going except you."

"Oh, Benjamin," Claire said. Her eyes were bright. "I'm so *glad*."

"I'm glad for you, too," he said. "About Sean. That

it's over. Did you call the hospital this morning?"

"No."

"I did," Benjamin said gently. "He's listed as stable."

Claire was about to say something when Nina and Burke came over. Burke jingled the car keys. "You ready, Claire?"

"Sure."

"Are you going, too?" Benjamin asked Nina.

"I can't," Nina said. "Because the car is too full of Claire's junk. Dad can't even put the seat back. Wait until you see him behind the wheel. He looks like a cockroach driving a matchbox."

"Nina," Burke said with weary patience, "*how* do I look like a cockroach driving a matchbox?"

Nina gave Benjamin a knowing look. "Just wait until you see it."

"Come on," Burke said. "Hug each other good-bye, and let's get going."

"We don't hug," both girls replied.

"You *have* to hug," Benjamin said. "Claire's going off to college." He hugged Claire briefly to demonstrate.

"We're conditioned not to hug," Nina said. "When I was an infant, Claire knocked me out of the cradle, and after that my parents always said, *Claire! No touch baby!*"

"Nina," Burke said, shocked. "That is absolutely not true."

"No, but I wish it were," Nina said cheerfully.

"Come on, Dad, let's go," Claire said. She picked up a big cardboard box.

Nina opened the passenger door for Claire just as the breeze picked up and blew Claire's hair into her eyes. Nina reached out and pushed the hair behind Claire's ears. They smiled briefly at each other. "Now, be—" Nina began, but broke off in annoyance. "Benjamin, stop taking our picture!"

"Sorry."

Claire settled into the car and rolled down the window. Burke started the engine. "Bye," Claire said as they pulled away.

"Good-bye!" Nina shouted, standing on her toes to wave. "I was about to say, 'Be careful! They *burn* witches in Massachusetts!'"

Jake stood awkwardly with Kate and her mother by Mrs. Levin's rented car. Kate's long red hair was blowing in the wind like a banner. He shook hands with Kate's mother.

"Good-bye," he said formally.

"Good-bye, Jake," Mrs. Levin said. "Thank you for—all you've done."

It seemed so silly put like that, as though his whole relationship with Kate was a favor he'd done for a friend. Jake didn't want to say, "You're welcome," so he said nothing. He put his hands in his pockets. Mrs. Levin got in the car and shut the door.

Jake turned to Kate. "You sure you know what you're doing?"

Kate pulled her sweater around her and smiled faintly. "Yes," she said. "This is the right thing for me now, Jake. Trust me."

He cleared his throat. "Okay."

She slipped her arms around him, and he buried his lips in her hair. "Take—care of yourself."

"I love you, too," she said softly.

"Yes, that's what I meant," he said quickly, and they both smiled a little shakily and pulled apart. Jake looked at her face. "Hey, you're not even crying."

She shook her head. "That doesn't mean I'm not sad." Her small face was grave. "Good-bye, Jake."

"Good-bye." He stood back a little so she could open the car door.

She pulled the door shut and gave him a little smile, then searched for something in the glove compartment. By the time Mrs. Levin had pulled away, Kate was sitting up and looking out the windshield—looking forward, Jake realized, into a future that didn't include him.

"So where *is* Zoey?" Aisha whispered to Nina. "I can't believe she didn't come to say good-bye to any of us."

"She's—" Nina felt her lower lip begin to

tremble. "Eesh"—her eyes welled up with tears—"I can't . . ."

"Okay, okay," Aisha said soothingly. "I'll call you after Christopher drops me off, all right? Tonight?"

Nina nodded.

"Now hug me good-bye," Aisha instructed.

Nina wrapped her arms around Aisha's thin frame and smelled her unique mixture of soap and perfume and bran muffins. She closed her eyes. Aisha squeezed her. "It'll be okay," she whispered.

She released Nina and hugged and kissed her parents. Then she gathered the squirming Kalif up in her arms and kissed his forehead twice. "Good-bye," she whispered. "Thank you for giving me my tape."

Kalif wiggled away from her, looking distinctly embarrassed.

"Well, we're off, I guess," Aisha said, reaching for Christopher's hand. "I'll call everyone as soon as I have a phone and a phone number. Good-bye!"

"Good-bye!" everyone said.

They watched as Aisha and Christopher climbed into the Grays' overloaded station wagon and drove out of the parking lot, Aisha at the wheel. The back window of the station wagon was open so that a big potted plant could stick out, its leaves rustling merrily in the wind. It seemed to Nina that even the plant was waving good-bye to her, even the plant was happy to be leaving.

Nina really had nothing but the utmost admiration for Mr. and Ms. Passmore. Really.

First, although Nina knew that they must have *some* idea of what had made Zoey leave early, they had been warm and friendly to both Nina and Lucas. And not asked any questions.

And now they were strolling hand in hand around the parking lot, chatting easily and politely not looking at the spectacle of Nina sobbing in Benjamin's arms.

"Nina?" Benjamin said, stroking her hair. "Take it easy."

"I can't!" she sobbed. "Oh, Benjamin, I can't believe you know! Who told you?"

He didn't stop stroking her hair. "Does it matter?"

"Yes!"

"Zoey told me. Before she left."

Nina cried harder.

"Nina," Benjamin said gently. "Come on."

Nina looked up at him. Her gray eyes were red and swollen. "Do—do you hate me?" she whispered.

"Don't be silly."

She wiped her nose on the sleeve of her rugby shirt. "That's not an answer."

Benjamin smiled. "Then the answer is no. I

don't hate you. I could never hate you, Nina."

"Oh, Benjamin." She leaned her head against his chest.

"Hey, I thought you were just about through," he protested.

She shook her head. "I'm just getting started."

"Nina?" a voice said tentatively. It was Lucas. "We should go. The ferry's almost ready to leave."

Nina kept her face hidden.

"He's right," Benjamin said. "You have to catch the ferry, and I have to go. Besides, my parents have walked around the parking lot five times, and now my father is explaining something about Dumpster construction to my mother, but I don't know how long he can make that last."

Nina gave him a faint watery smile.

"Good girl," Benjamin said, releasing her.

He shook hands with Lucas. "It'll be okay," he said.

Lucas smiled sardonically. "You mean Zoey's going to forgive me?"

Benjamin looked pained. "Zoey—"

"Never mind; I shouldn't have asked," Lucas said. "See you at Thanksgiving."

"Thanks," Benjamin said. "Good-bye, Lucas. Good-bye, Nina."

He leaned down suddenly and kissed Nina, a real kiss—long, passionate, public.

Oh, Nina thought breathlessly. *That's just how I*

imagined he would kiss me when he left for college. That's just how I imagined it when I had a crush on him for all those years. And he must have known.

"Good-bye!" she called as he walked across the parking lot. "Good-bye, Benjamin!"

She wrapped her arms around herself and stood next to Lucas, shivering. Together they watched Benjamin and the Passmores climb into their car and drive away.

"Lucas?" Nina said after a moment.

"What?" he asked.

There were so many things she wanted to say. She paused.

"Nothing," she said.

He looked at her a moment. Then they turned and walked toward the ferry.

The photograph Benjamin took of Nina and Claire shows two girls looking at each other with intense, if fleeting, tenderness. Nina's fingers are touching Claire's cheek as gently as they might stroke a butterfly's wing. Benjamin wanted to frame it and send it to Claire, but somehow he never got around to it. He kept it for himself instead.

It was a perfect example of the kind of thing one missed in a world of darkness.

The twenty-fifth title in the fabulous MAKING OUT series:

Don't forget Lara. As if anyone could! She's lied, schemed and manipulated herself into everyone's lives. But now she's turning her own life around, and it feels great. There's only one problem – the terrifying dreams that haunt her sleep.

Don't forget Lara